C000098913

Praise for Tar

For: My Mother Was An Upright Piano

Tania Hershman writes with such passion and playfulness, the pain and the fear and the hope woven through her stories hits all the harder. The result is beautiful, funny and quietly devastating."
Nicola Walker, actress

"The writer Alasdair Gray once described himself as "a maker of imagined objects." It strikes me that Tania Hershman needs a more artful descriptor than 'writer,' too: brilliant; mysterious; not of this earth—I adore her and I adore this book."
Marjorie Celona, author, Y

"Funny, fresh, lyrical. These stories are like colorful glass lozenges holding the substance of our everyday lives, sparkled up by the unusual and wondrous."
Aimee Bender, author of Willful Creatures and The Particular Sadness of Lemon Cake

"Her presentation of the tragedy and the oddity of our human lives is the typed equivalent of a performance artist at MOMA: strange, unfamiliar, captivating. The universe's dark energy palpitates on Hershman's pages; she gives emptiness form. Characters struggle to communicate, to make themselves known to others. Hopes for the world to be other than it is are met with silence. Longing blankets the text. Sentences stop before they reach their conclusion, words omitted by the author in sympathy with the reticence of her fictional creations. The unsaid contains both dagger and salve, and Hershman's silences both break and heal the heart." *Kerry Shadid, World Literature Today*

For: The White Road and Other Stories

"Inspired by scientific progress and science journalism, including articles in New Scientist, and driven by an author dripping with talent, this is as good as modern reading gets." *Michael Brooks, New Scientist magazine*

"Perhaps the most satisfying element of The White Road & Other Stories (and this could be the secret key to successful short stories the world over), Hershman has a keen mind, can concoct the sort of slippery knot that hooks you, that has you turning pages to see what happens next (which is rare in short story land, or at least in the short story land I've visited)" *Bookmunch*

"The eponymous story of this collection is worth the price of admission. It is, without a doubt, one of the best short stories I've ever read. A woman, at the end of the world, who has endured the loss of a child but more than that, seen his dead body, that death from his own hand, and so she finds a way to see nothing but bright white ever again. I was genuinely moved and shocked by this story. So remarkable.....The one constant through each of these stories is the care Hershman has taken with her characters. This was a collection that was written with love." *Roxane Gay, PANK magazine*

"Hershman is an interested, dreaming science observer who pays serious and at times myopic attention to sci-tech news stories and considers what they might mean...."
Amy Charles, LabLit

Tania Hershman is a former science journalist living and working in the UK. Her first short story collection, The White Road and Other Stories (Salt Publishing), was commended by the judges of the 2009 Orange Award for New Writers. She is also the author of the poetry collection Terms and Conditions (Nine Arches Press, 2017), My Mother Was An Upright Piano: Fictions (Tangent Books, 2012), Nothing Here Is Wild, Everything Is Open (Southword Editions, 2016), and co-author of Writing Short Stories: A Writers and Artists Companion (Bloomsbury, 2014). Tania is founder and curator of ShortStops, www.shortstops.info, the UK & Ireland short story hub.

Visit Tania's website www.taniahershman, follow her on twitter @taniahershman, and listen to her read her work at www.soundcloud.com/taniahershman/

First published in Great Britain 2017
Text copyright © 2017 Tania Hershman
The moral right of the author has been asserted

Unthank Books
PO Box 3506
Norwich
NR7 7QP
www.unthankbooks.com

A CIP catalogue record for this book is avail-
able from the British Library

Any resemblance to persons fictional or real
who are living, dead, or undead, is purely
coincidental

Typesetting by Silly Spaceman

ISBN 978-1-910061-48-0

Some of Us Glow More Than Others

stories

by Tania Hershman

Contents

Ordinary people are peculiar too:
Watch the vagrant in their eyes
Who sneaks away while they are talking with you
Into some black wood behind the skull,
Following un-, or other, realities,
Fishing for shadows in a pool.

From *Conversation* by Louis MacNeice

Grounded

"It ends with the woman, birds tapping at the window, smiling."

It Begins With Birds in Flight

It begins with birds in flight, with birds landing, taking off, and she, the woman, watching trees at the city's edge. It begins with watching birds, in the trees, and in its middle, later, there is a kitchen, and the woman stands, the teakettle's small hard tears of water dripping onto her fingers. The woman stands, the kitchen waits, the birds have gone, and the house, struck by the finery of a silent, standing woman, takes itself out for a spell. The woman pours, the kettle's whistle quiet now. It ends with the woman, sitting, fine and silent, sitting, straight and awkward, angles and corners pointing towards the sides. It ends with birds, tapping on the window, tapping and scratching, and the woman, her head up, her tea aside. It ends with the woman, birds tapping at the window, smiling.

Missing My Liar

Am I missing my liar? she says. What was the last lie? she says. Oh yes, she says, I remember. That was the car, she says. A bad lie, she says, outbreathing. Broken bones and healed bones and eyes stitched shut. Am I missing my liar? Am I? Is no-one safe? And she gets in her new car and leaves.

The next week, the same questions. Are you missing your liar yet? Am I? She says. Is my liar here? she says, looking around, under and behind. Is there room for a liar here? What was the lie before that? Oh yes, the cat, that lie was not a broken-bones lie. The cat came back. The cat found its way. I am not missing my liar yet. And she stands up, leaves a cheque, and walks away.

It takes six months. Am I missing my liar? she says and this time: Yes. Everything is too truthy. Everything is just right there where it is, as it is. My liar added worlds. My liar turned life coloured. She cries when she says this. My liar hurt me, cheated, stole from me. I miss my liar. I miss, I miss, I miss. And she curls around and fits herself into the couch, bones sewing together and her eyes cemented.

A Song for Falling

She composed. A song for standing, a song for sitting. A suite of songs for bathing. Two songs she could not choose between for cookery. She was working on a song for falling from a great height – when he did.

And then she could not finish it.

She took all her songs and put them in the fridge. To make space, the vegetables – tomatoes and raw carrots - she spread out on the summer lawn.

She found she could not cry. She had no song yet for grief, she had thought herself too young. She had thought. Or not thought. And now she wished she had stared down at her falling song and considered. Why why why.

No more songs came, and the ones in the fridge curled around themselves, volcanic dust finding its way in to cover them.

When the grass on the lawn grew so that it hid her, hid her vegetables, almost hid the sun, a note appeared. Inside her head, which had been dry as Yellowstone. A song. Only a small small song. Only a song for breathing, for taking the next breath.

She would wait. Now that one had come, she was less un-sure about a song for getting up, a song for moving through tall grass, a song for reentering the house. A song for how to live now that you know what life can do to you.

God Glows

Mother Superior agrees to fund Emmylene's equipment.

"Science is so soothing," she says, her deep voice making it sound biblical.

Soothing? thinks Emmylene, almost tempted, once again, to blaspheme. Memories of frogs' bodies slit open for prying fingers and the shrieking of one girl who vomited violently. Not so much, she thinks.

"Pouring from one test tube to the other, the elements of life," says Mother Superior. Emmylene sees that faraway look in her eyes.

"Yes," she says. "Soothing. I'll go and place the order."

"Thank you, Sister Morris. Bless your endeavours." Mother Superior sits back behind her desk and Emmylene goes to phone the supplier.

Emmylene used to be a physicist. She had thought that was a calling. Then there was another sort, and here she is in a world of women.

On the phone, she orders test tubes in various sizes, with racks, rockers, a heating bath, a freezer and a fridge. A machine for gel electrophoresis. Several timers and pipettes. Lab coats, tweezers, syringes, a confocal microscope – the most expensive item. And a cage of knockout mice.

"Sister Morris," she tells the salesgirl and gives the address.

"Convent?" says the salesgirl.

"Yes," says Emmylene, imagining her bench, her test tube racks, her mice.

She had subscribed to *Cell* and *Nature Biology*, with Mother Superior's permission.

"God glows," Mother Superior had said when shown images of immune cells lit up in green and red.

Emmylene likes to walk the convent grounds with letters from a biochemist friend who still writes to her about his experiments. "Dear Emmylene," she reads while sitting on a chair-shaped rock by the river, "I'm coming closer to understanding this pathway. My zebrafish were problematic for a while but now the mutants are breeding well. I've been working on the wild type in the meantime."

She loves the words: Lamellipodia, organelles, green fluorescent protein, mcherry. Sometimes they slip into her prayers: "Blessed are the macrophages," "Our heavenly lymphocytes". She opens her eyes, looks around the chapel at her kneeling sisters. I am strange, thinks Emmylene.

When the lab equipment arrives, Emmylene needs Sister John and Sister Immelda's help to set it up. Sister Immelda giggles every time a new package is opened.

"What does that do?" she asks again and again. Sister John shushes her.

"We will find out," says Sister John, unwrapping a pipette.

Emmylene is happier than she can remember. She arranges her bench like the first day of school: one bright pink test tube rack, three pipettes in a line. Her lab coat, so white, so unstained.

"Will you wear it over...?" says Sister Immelda, who, Emmylene can see, is on the brink of a "me too" moment.

"Probably," she says, wanting not to try it on now, but later. On her own.

The knockout mice are coming separately. She isn't sure how that's done. And then. She's watched videos. But Emmylene still isn't convinced she'll be able to do it.

When Sister John takes Sister Immelda off to the vegetable garden, Emmylene tries on the lab coat over her habit. She ordered extra large but it feels odd, too bulky to do any work in. She shuts the door, slips out of her habit and puts it on over her underwear. At that instant she remembers the kiss. That kiss. Closing her eyes, there are lips on hers, in a car park, they are sixteen or seventeen. He's kissing her. More gently than she'd thought, and then he licks her earlobe and the wave that swept through her then floods her again. She lowers her head onto the cool bench.

Emmylene has decided to extract some DNA. She has sent off for a line of HeLa cells, and is following the protocol she printed out. There are so many steps. It has to be done slowly, otherwise she'll ruin it and she doesn't have large quantities of anything. She keeps telling herself it's like a recipe, but really it isn't. Making a cake, you can see the ingredients: here is flour, these are eggs. But this is all clear liquid, one poured into another, stirred, rocked, frozen, thawed, stirred, left, stirred. It takes hours.

When Emmylene comes up for air, her test tubes set to rock for 90 minutes, she has a stiff neck and her hands are sore from gripping the pipette. She puts her habit back on and goes for a walk, clipping the digital timer to her belt. There hasn't been a letter for a while, not from anyone. Her mother writes occasionally but prefers email. Emmylene was surprised by the biochemist's regular correspondence, on paper too. There was never anything between us, she thinks, sitting on the chair-shaped rock. Was there? Is he? But I'm a nun.

"I'm a nun," she says out loud, to the trees and whoever might be listening. Fuck me, she thinks, then takes hold of her cross and kisses it. The timer beeps. Her cells need her.

It hasn't worked. Ten hours and nothing happened. Ten hours of following each step as carefully as possible, with brand new equipment. Emmylene is despairing.

"Never mind," says Sister John, passing the potatoes. "It's just your first try."

"Physics wasn't like this," says Emmylene. "Physics is so different, there's more thinking and planning, and you can't see things either but somehow there's more knowing. I don't know."

"How did you do it?" says Sister Immelda, who is very very young, who became a nun before she had become a woman. Emmylene sometimes wonders what kind of woman Sister Immelda would have been, out there. The word "stripper" comes into her head; Sister Immelda is quite gorgeous. Emmylene will have to ask forgiveness for that later, as she often does. Her thoughts trip her up daily, hourly.

"You're trained, you learn the language, and really, to be

honest, if you don't get it quite early on, it's never going to happen," says Emmylene, spearing a pea. Physics had been neat and tidy, she had been one of the chosen ones who did see, who lived in that country. Damn.

"I don't think I ever could have," says Sister Immelda, buttering a piece of bread. "I'm not clever enough." Emmylene looks up and stares at the girl.

"Don't say that," Emmylene says. "Never say that," and then, for a moment, she thinks she might cry. "Excuse me," she says, pushing her chair back. Outside in the cold corridor she does cry, without knowing why. No-one hears her. No-one comes out.

Emmylene's mice arrive. There are four, white with red eyes.

"Hello, my little mutants," Emmylene whispers to them as she looks around her lab for the right place. They stare back, seemingly stunned by their journey. Emmylene still doesn't quite know how mice are transported, and it feels callous to just phone up and order animals. How far could it go? Lions, tigers? Monkeys, probably, with the right kind of permits. She imagines a chimpanzee with electrodes sticking from his skull. No. Not that.

She reads the care instructions again and feeds her mice, resisting the urge to pick one up and stroke it. The mice eat, then vanish within the mounds of hay in their cage.

Emmylene sits, fiddling with a pipette's volume adjuster. When the word "Mendel" comes into her head, she is startled. And then she understands. He had his peas, she has her lab. Father Gregor.

It is as Emmylene is wandering through the woods behind the convent that she wonders if Mother Superior
would allow her to take blood. From everyone, it would be
easily done. But this might be stepping over some line. This
kind of science, she imagines Mother Superior saying, is not
as soothing as I had imagined. This is what I had feared,
we are all to be your test subjects, Sister Morris. Emmylene
rehearses responses in her head, sitting on a flat stone by the
river. She tries to conjure the spirit of Mendel, but he cross-
bred plants. She suspects that won't help her argument.

She starts to write to her biochemist friend, while wearing her lab coat, watched by her red-eyed mice. Emmylene
wants to ask him. She is not sure what exactly. Something
about the essence of it, but then all that is in her head are
quarks, bosons, neutrinos, from her old country. She puts
her pen down. The mice scurry.

"What are you so busy doing?" she says. Then she undoes the top button of her lab coat, scratches her neck. Emmylene yawns. She thinks again of Mendel and she wonders
what her own purpose might be. God? Emmylene makes
herself ask the question. She says it aloud: "What would
God want me to do?" but then she can't bring herself to
accept that God might want her, as Sister Morris or as Emmylene, to do anything at all. Or anything more than getting
up every morning, stretching into the darkness of the day.
Just that act. Which still so often feels like an achievement.

Later, Emmylene makes a list in her notebook. She puts

down "taking blood" and then a dash, and that space, the one following the dash, seems to scream at her. Why? it shouts. Why blood? What for? What would you do with all that blood? Why would you take needles, look at their arms, look at their skin. Puncture. Puncture. The word rolls around her mind. Sharpness. A stab.

The first experiment that works is one that Emmylene learns from watching a video online. A very simple thing, although even "simple" takes two days, looking for a particular gene that she knows is definitely activated in the mice. Emmylene watches the film – which shows only the researcher's purple-gloved hands and part of their torso – five times. She watches those hands move, listens to the voice, which is American, which she finds hard to assign a gender to. The flash of the fingers, the pipetting, comforts her. A memory comes of the physics lab, a similar soothing, a falling back towards something that will catch you, always. Emmylene's stomach, her knees, her earlobes, ache with missing it. She undoes a button of her lab coat while she waits for something to defrost. Swivelling her chair around, she undoes another, rubs underneath her left bra strap. She had thought never to wear one again, here. But she has not been able. To let that go.

When it works, when the results are developed and there is the line, there is the gene, Emmylene notices that she doesn't feel the way she expected. "Is this how it is for you?" she asks her biochemist friend inside her head. All Emmylene is is tired. She wriggles out of the lab coat and stands for a while in her underwear. The mice scurry.

That night at dinner, Sister Immelda is staring at her. Emmylene keeps eating, then looks up again. Sister Immelda hasn't touched any of her food. She seems to be trying to send Emmylene an urgent message, her eyes wide. Emmylene raises her eyebrows. Sister Immelda looks around, then leans across the table.

"Can I talk to you? After?" she says, and Emmylene sees that Sister Immelda's normally pearly skin is pale and under her eyes are patches of darkness. Emmylene nods, looks back down. Peas. Peas. Father Gregor. She doesn't tell anyone about her result. She doesn't know what to say.

In the garden behind the convent, by the rose bushes, Sister Immelda cries. Emmylene stands beside her, not touching, unsure. Sister Immelda's crying is noisy, uncontrolled, and Emmylene stares at a large yellow rose just behind Immelda's head, a rose which any moment might weep its own petals. Immelda sways and grips onto Emmylene's arm so suddenly she is shocked, a spasm running through her.

"Sorry, sorry, sorry," gulps Immelda, gasping.

"It's okay," says Emmylene, although it may not be. "Do you want...?" And then she finds that Immelda is hugging her with a strength that Emmylene would never have imagined.

"I can't," Immelda whispers into Emmylene's ear. "I can't."

"Neither can I," thinks Emmylene and then there is that pit and there is only down. She blinks. "Come and see my mice," she says, and leads Sister Immelda away from the rose bush, from the thorns.

14

Sister Immelda visits Emmylene in her laboratory often after that. She is still pale, her eyes have dark moons now, but she smiles and she talks to the mice.

"Don't give them names," says Emmylene.

"Too late!"

"Oh dear," says Emmylene, knowing anyway that she could never kill them, even though that, she has heard from the biochemist, is an essential part of the job. She watches Immelda stretch towards the cage and slide one finger through to let a curious mouse sniff. She looks at Immelda's forearm. Emmylene wonders if.

"Would you...?" she says, and when Immelda agrees, Emmylene realises she will have to watch another video to learn how to. This is not peas, she thinks.

Once the needle goes in and Immelda's blood starts to flow into the tube, Emmylene relaxes.

"Okay?" she says. Immelda grins. She appears to be enjoying this immensely.

"Vampires," says Immelda. "Always had a bit of a thing for them... I don't know." She giggles and then they both do. And then they're laughing so hard Emmylene thinks she might choke. The mice scrabble.

When it's done, they sit and look at the four tubes of Immelda's blood in the test tube rack.

"I'll take mine too," says Emmylene.

"What will you do with it all?" says Immelda, pressing the cotton wool onto her arm. Emmylene doesn't know how to answer. It's no more than a feeling right now. But the sight of those test tubes makes her happy. "No pressure," says Immelda, and laughs. They hear the bell for supper. Immelda waves to the mice as they leave.

A letter. From the biochemist. But this time, for the first time, he doesn't talk about biochemistry, about his work. He seems to be opening his heart to Emmylene. It's because I'm safe, Emmylene tells herself, sitting on her chair-shaped rock. I'm a nun. And she looks up into the trees, at a bird, who flies off. The biochemist has had his heart broken, mangled, by someone he met at a conference. His sentences are twisted, as if she, this other biochemist, has torn something, wrecked some mechanism. Emmylene has never read a letter that made her feel so uneasy. She has to keep stopping to look out over the river, to breathe. "Everything I study is useless," writes the biochemist. "Fuck science, fuck scientific enquiry." I'm a nun, thinks Emmylene, and remembers Immelda's forearm, the syringe.

Emmylene is testing the blood. She has hers and she has Immelda's, carefully and separately labelled. She has watched no videos, read no protocols. There are no videos or protocols for this. The mice, bolder, stare at her. Emmylene is looking for. Looking. For.

Looking.

Emmylene works through two meals. She stops only to stand, to stretch her neck, lift both arms up above her head. No-one comes. Even Immelda doesn't visit. As if they know what she needs, what she doesn't need. Emmylene finds herself carrying on past dark, missing prayers. And still no-one comes.

The nuns are sat in rows and she, Emmylene, Sister Morris, is facing them.

"I…," she says. The sisters beam, nod, encourage.

Emmylene looks to the back wall then up to the ceiling, stretching her stiff neck, her sore hands. She is wearing her lab coat. She thought about putting it on over her habit but when she tried it again as she had that first day, it was even worse, even bulkier. Inauthentic. So she is wearing it next to her skin. She wonders if the nuns can see through it, through her. But they are all still smiling, waiting, and so Emmylene assumes she is not improper. Yet.

"I've found…," she says, and switches on the Power-Point. There is a gasp. Sister Immelda gives her the thumbs-up, grinning.

On the screen, or rather on the white white convent wall that the computer is projecting onto, is an image of cells. Emmylene tagged them so that what she has discovered is painted red, bright lipstick red.

"Here," says Emmylene. Sister Morris.

The sisters stare at her. Immelda tilts her head to the side as if to say, Go on. Go on.

"Here," says Emmylene again. "Right here." And she moves to the wall, puts her finger up against the pulsing red.

"What are they?" asks Sister John.

"I took…," says Emmylene, then stops, looks at Mother Superior. Mother Superior's expression is open, curious. "I took blood. From myself, and Sister Immelda. With her consent, of course." Mother Superior's face has not changed. Emmylene feels bolder. "I didn't know what I was looking

17

for. And that's not scientific. In science, you need a hypothesis, an idea, a theory, first. Then you test it. Well, you try and disprove it, really. Falsification. Try every way you can to be wrong. To make it wrong. Try to break it."

"Yes," says one of the older nuns, who has been in the convent for longer than Emmylene has been alive. "Break it," murmurs the elderly woman, and Emmylene sees her tap her fingers gently on the arm of the sister sitting next to her.

"I didn't," says Emmylene. "I had no theory, no idea what I wanted to search for. So instead, I took blood, our blood, then just looked and looked at it, under the microscope. That's when I found it."

"Sister Morris," says Mother Superior in her deep voice, and Emmylene jumps, feeling as if she has been caught out by a teacher. But Mother Superior is smiling. "You are keeping us most wonderfully in suspense, child. What have you discovered, in the blood?"

"Love," whispers Emmylene, and her hands find each other, fingers knitting together, and she is crying. And then she is surrounded by nuns, who come up to her, who rise from their seats to encircle her, Sister Immelda closest, arms around her neck.

In the car park, two people are kissing. A boy is kissing a girl. A girl is being kissed. Later, that girl is in a lecture theatre, taking notes on electro-magnetic fields, numbers and Greek letters. Even later still, that girl is standing in a room being held tightly, so tightly, that even if she sways, even if she gets dizzy, her knees buckling, she will not fall.

What Is It That Fills Us

A song for the last of the gasometers*

They first suggested relocation. They did this out of love, wanting to avoid dismantlement, demolition. All but one agreed; the final one said,

– Not without my gas.

– But… they said. But we don't know how to…

Silence.

They went away, drew up plans and schemas, wondered and attempted. They did this out of love. They wanted to avoid dismantlement, demolition. But they had no ideas. No solution.

One of them went back alone, to ask directly.

– How? She said to the gas, as it rustled, shifted, so that she never spoke to the same molecule twice. How do we move you? Then she waited, listened, opened herself up. But all she heard was a whispering, a hissing, as if the gas molecules were suspicious.

She fell asleep. When she woke up, the gas, all the gas, was gone. Then, the final one agreed to leave.

Now they stand in rows, but they are empty. Each one of their hearts is broken.

*Gas holders, sometimes known as gasometers, began to emerge in Britain in Victorian times and do largely as the name suggests: store large volumes of gas, usually from nearby gasworks. National Grid revealed plans to demolish 76 gas holders and now Southern and Scottish Gas networks have revealed plans to tear down 111 gas holders.

Biography (ongoing)

At 100 she looked back. Each decade a new discovery. Ten Nobel prizes, she built a house around them, as reporters snaked across the lawn. First physics, then biology, and in each lab someone proposed marriage. She turned them all down then turned back to her bench, her fume cupboard, her centrifuge. At forty she became an inorganic chemist; at fifty she took to aeronautical design. At sixty she sighed, but at sixty-one, pressed on. Retirement came and went. Asked at 89, did she have regrets, she laughed and laughed, then took up molecular gastronomy. She's still going strong.

Burrowing Blind

The first one they blinded bumped and banged her way through the burrow, emerging bruised, blinking. Bad one, they said. The blinding's off, we need to try again. They sent the first one to the cafeteria, feeling her way along walls, crawling down stairs, dipping fingers in other people's coffee, and there she sat and wept, the large cheque sitting, stained, on the table.

The second one was better, sensing sounds without background burbling and backbiting. Look at her, they said, she's properly moling, and they proudly watched and proudly grinned and when she was sent downstairs after, she was prouder too, although feeling her way along walls, hearing cups crash and coffee gurgle.

Five more later they had blinding down to a tee, no more calibration fuck-ups. We've our moles, they smirked and slapped backs and called bosses and alerted newsmen and newswomen, and the moles were aligned and photographed, blinking and feeling the air.

The three-mole labour force dispatched did engage and retrieve but this was only minimal retrieval and though successful was not enough for bosses frowning and demanding, and so the larger pack was given the toughest of all and sent far, far underground. Despite extended and extensive silence training one mole could not but cough and sneeze until her nearest colleague shut her down with a swift shot. No time for remorse, regret, they burrowed on, one mole short but still equipped enough.

For years the moling squad did burrow beneath and bring back treasures of one sort or another, sometimes breathing ones, thwarting thugs and terrorists, and sometimes painted ones, great works of art that had wandered, and sometimes items they couldn't name at all, even when one mole shook it and the others, deep deep underground, strained to hear. There was little they could not tackle, but when they surfaced they were never sure what day or time it was or where the door might be and they bumbled, fumbled, happy only when below.

When it came time to retire, the moles were again aligned and photographed, blinking and feeling the air, and then carried off to the countryside where they were dumped in dusty chairs and in their dreams relived the great retrievals. One night when summoned, no moles arrived for supper, and carers checked their rooms to find the holes through which the squad had bashed back down to where they belonged.

No-one saw the moles again, but every few years there is a photo, on television, the internet and newspapers, of the old mole squad, proudly medalled, blinking. Blind as bats, as toads, as dark-eyed sloths, they saved the day.

Fight Or Flight

"Your fingers closed around her bones and felt the bird, wings beating, beating."

Switchgirls

We had one each, assigned upon reaching a certain age. I cannot be certain now, given my current age, what that age was. I am so old now, so so old, it is a wonder I recall anything at all. Those switches on the wall, they were so much to me, mother and father to me.

Where was I?

I was the youngest, of course. Only the youngest would be recording this now, the elder ones having gone off to live their lives, in ways the youngest never can.

Switch it up. Switch it down. On/Off. Off/On.

She never spoke to me. She flung her hands towards me every now and every then, signals I learned, fast, because if not the slaps came next. And when she was up, she was as if on fire, a firework, spinning and wheeling, burning, singeing. I, the smallest, the littlest, the slowest to move out of reach, stuck in my daydreaming. She was my sister. What kind of sister? A sister I was to her, a slave sister. The others ran and danced away, pinching me as they left me to fetch, carry, brush, comb.

Switch it up. Switch it down. On/Off. Off/On.

There are stories I can tell of her, the Upper Sister, how she pressed me to the wall beside our switches, held my neck in such a way that marks are still there, patterns from the wall-paper impressed into my skin. She was violence, she was un-stopped, being that we had no-one above us, no one to tame us.

They made her wrong, I know now, after all these years. She was the first, and the mix was flawed, oh how flawed it was! She could not speak, was that not the first sign? Should They not have done for her early on? Perhaps They were then too young too, too naïve about Their methods.

The others, less flawed, less cruel, left me with her. I was the basest rung, the step she climbed upon. Oh sister.

Switch it up. Switch it down. On/Off. Off/On.

The Middle two were pretty little things, but they still had some glitches. One had an eye that would not stay still; the other fluttering hands that men found oh so lovely until they tried to settle her, when wooing would not even make her unmove. And what was wrong with me? Perhaps only that I did not know that nothing was. I was Their success, They must have jumped up and down, They must have laughed when They made me, I know that now. Yes! They will have said to one another.

(I know not how many There were then, or how many now are left, if any at all. It has been so long since They, since any of Them, came…)

Switch it up. Switch it down. On/Off. Off/On.

And what of the switches? When I said mother's milk, did

I say mother's milk, I cannot remember, but I meant it, all that we knew of mothers was from those switches. Nudge yours slightly slowly up and it would flood you, flood *me*, with happy. Our happy switch, when up – but limited. I imagine Them writing charts, setting boundaries, No, no, they must not be allowed happy-all-the-time. No. No. A set amount, that's all. And each switch was sacredly connected in to one of us, I had mine, the two Middle girls had theirs and she, my Upper Sister, must have had hers too. But my Upper Sister never switched, so far as I could see, because to slap and bother me, to order me about, did it for her enough. Enough. Happy-all-the-time.

Switch it up. Switch it down. On/Off. Off/On.

The last time I recall They came to see us, I was just coming off a happy. I beamed and beamed at Them as They took notes, scribbled into small machines. Upper Sister was still there, our Middle two had both found switchmen to make homes with. Just me and her, her wildly swinging arms not aged, not slowed.

I don't know when They took her. Sometime on that visit, maybe. Maybe I turned around, maybe They happied me up with some fancy tricks, but when I unhappied back I was alone.

I do sometimes re-hear some words They said: Expedience. Survive. Functionality. But there were no instructions left, notes pinned on no walls for me. Alone.

Switch it up. Switch it down. On/Off. Off/On.

There was someone once. He did a little create some happy for me. But when he moved his arms towards my face, my neck, my legs, I was flinching and twitching and seeing her, the Upper Sister, back there, and no amount of time would change that, so he walked away. And the Middle Sisters do not contact, do not message, do not come back to see how all has never changed but me older and older.

Switch it up. Switch it down. On/Off. Off/On.

Why I am all about this now, with me so ancient? It is this: Mother's milk is almost gone. I nudge and flick my own switch, and even chance the others too, but I get just a shiver, just a tiny slip of happy now and the shivers and the slips are less and less.

Do I imagine Them, still in Their rooms, still watching, cutting down my daily limits, saying, Let's see if she... ?

I more imagine that I have outlived Them all, that I was not supposed to be on and on and on the way I have. They made me so well, I am so *perfect*, I am still here. But. But. When there is not a drop of happy left what will I do?

I am imagining that: the ways They might have imagined for my ending. Maybe the happys were not just that, maybe are they fuel to fuel my thoughts, my arms and legs and other parts? And now there is no more but just a drop.

Switch it up. Switch it down. On/Off. Off/On.
I flick, a tiny slip, a tiny happy.

Switch it up. Switch it down. On/Off. Off/On.
Something. Maybe, something. So so small.

Switch it up. Switch it down. On/Off. Off/On.
Switch it up. Switch it down. On/Off. Off/On.
Switch it up. Switch it down. On/Off. Off/On.
Off/On.
Off/On.

Off.

Fine As Feathers

What do you want, he said. The way he looked at me. What do you want? He said it again as if maybe I hadn't heard.

Cut short, I said.

Pale skin, he said. Light brown hair.

Cut short, I said. Fine as feathers.

His face was an old oil painting, his eyes were from some other century. And there I was, like a house with its beams exposed. He put out a hand and although I understood the transaction, understood that this was part of how it had to be, I winced. He said nothing. Scissors in one hand, his other hand hovered.

Fine as feathers, he said.

I think you will laugh at me, when I tell you about it. I think you'll go Freudian, talk about blades and skin and mutilation, sex and mother issues.

A hair cut, you say.

I felt, I say. I felt it had something more. He wasn't the usual. You know.

Effeminate, you say, and smirk. You smirk as if you know all this better than I do.

I didn't want to use that word, I say, and turn to look through the window into the street because you aren't being nice, and I need you to be nice. Because you have a cruelty in you that comes through when what I need is kindness.

He raised his scissors and I closed my eyes. As I sat there I heard a bird and the sound came closer. The bird was singing, and the motion of him cutting, of him severing the ends, fitted in with the bird's odd sounds. As if he and the bird were dancing and my hair was dancing with them. Even though my eyes were shut, I saw this bird, its great plumage, its red throat. I saw him turn to the bird, still cutting my hair. And then I was outside and looking in at myself. And then I was the bird.

You have very little difficulty interpreting the dream. I know you think you sound sympathetic. I know you think you sound a great many things.

You are full of fear, you say to me. You long for wings, you long for your chains to be cut.

You are smug.

But who is he? I say, looking at you, looking into you as if to beg for something more like me, something more familiar.

He's just a conduit, you say.

What if he's God, I say, and then I wish I hadn't, I want to stuff the words back in.

Your look then is everything. Your look peels back my skin and I know we will never make it through this.

I was the bird then, and you were in the chair. He looked to me as if he wanted me to say something, to make some sound. I knew what he wanted. I opened my beak and it poured forth, and it came from something so deep inside, a sort of singing speech and so he cut and cut and cut some more. And then, when he had shorn your head, he moved the scissors closer. Closer to your neck, that pale blue vein. And you, looking in the mirror, didn't see. You, admiring, had a wall which kept out all danger. I knew, when he turned to me again, that he was asking me. All I had to give was a sign. The tip of the blade, right by your neck. Metal on skin.

Thin Ice

Her eyes, her eyes, blue like seaweed strangling a newborn. The smile like an animal trapped under thin ice that at any moment was cracking, gaping. You didn't know what to do with those eyes, that smile. You handed her the coffee and tried to look sympathetic.

"Sorry…about…," you said. You sat down, picked up your mug. She was warming hers, not drinking, not speaking. "Do you want to…?" Then, without you knowing what it was to be, you put down your mug and your hand reached for her wrist. Your fingers closed around her bones and felt the bird, wings beating, beating. And she turned up to you, as if your soft fingertips had found the lock and freed it. And she put down her coffee and dropped her other hand on yours, and you stayed there for a long time, as the sun moved across the sky.

War Games

A little girl, 10 or 11, smoking a cigarette, plays Monopoly on a beach while all around her, a war is raging. She never gets hit. Every now and then, a soldier will notice her and come and play a turn. If the soldier lands on certain places on the board, he gets transported there – Marylebone Station, for example - still in uniform. The child keeps playing, and smoking, and soldiers keep getting transported until there's only one left from each side. She invites them to join her. The one that isn't transported wins the war.

There are different ways to tell this story. We could land inside the child's head, as all around shells explode and she, taking another drag on her Marlboro, fiddles with her metal top hat, dog or miniature iron. You would need to know things then, given access to her brain. ("Shut up," says the child, "get out of here". "But why," you ask. "What are you doing here, you silly girl? Don't you know you might be…". "How do you know I'm not," sighs the child, inhaling.)

I could focus on in one soldier: How he sees the tiny girl, with her pack of cigarettes and her Zippo lighter. How she signals to him with a nod, how he watches as she blows smoke, how the smoke joins the pockmarked air. How she seems not to notice anything but him. "Play," she says, handing him the dog. He moves to take off his helmet but she looks impatient. "Play," she says, stubbing out a cigarette beneath the card table. (I have not mentioned the card table.

See, we're learning.) The soldier, most of his head still with his pals, twitching, looking around him where the action is, holds the dice. He scratches where his uniform is damp and sticks to him. The child lights another cigarette.

We could dive further inside our soldier, watch his synapses chatter as he takes in the scene. *Mother*, he is thinking. He has thought of his mother for most of the past hour and, for the few days before that, has had the smell of his favourite of her pies appearing and disappearing. "Do you smell…?" he kept asking Williams, his best friend, but Williams didn't, couldn't, wasn't able to smell much at all down here in this trench with the mud and the sweat and the rats that he dreamt of at night. Poor Williams. There goes half his skull.

The soldier puts down his piece on the starting square, then, as the girl watches him, rolls the dice. As he moves his metal dog along, the girl smiles. He is putting the dog down on Covent Garden when a shell explodes that makes the card table rattle. Our soldier looks up, startled, but the girl's hand presses on top of his on top of the dog on top of Covent Garden and, the shell's song still ringing in the air, he vanishes. (If I was to follow him, we would see him, that same instant, the ringing still in his ears, materialise by the market, by a flower stall, almost knocking down a bunch of daffodils. We would watch him stagger, grab the stall for support, the stallholder shouting "Oi, lad!" and then we would see him wander in a daze, looking around and back and around again, towards a pub on the corner, as the stallholder puts his daffodils back in order. But we don't follow him. Not yet.)

Let's go back to the girl, see what she does next. Why, the same again! With boys just from our side? No, no. Symmetrical.

I will tiptoe inside her head. She is singing. This tiny, smoking child, war all around, luring soldiers to Monopoly, is humming a lullaby to herself. Mother sang it to her, she remembers. But it didn't work. She was never soothed, this child. Not by songs, not by silence. She screamed and screamed and screamed.

Another soldier comes, another cigarette is lit, she doesn't offer him one, what a waste, he is only there – hand poised, dice rolled – for a few seconds, then off he goes, confused, to Waterloo Station.

Shall I take you into the heat of battle? It is not pretty in there. There is such a mess of bodies and a bloody carpet, I'd prefer to stand back. Let us be optimistic. Let us think of the soldiers suddenly appearing around London, a city most of them do not come from. The soldier sent most recently to Waterloo Station was the third to make it there in the space of thirty war minutes. But he does not see the others and they don't see him and no-one at all at the busy station notices.

Actually, this is a lie. (Did I promise you only one truth?) Someone has seen. But he, unfit for service, drinks to cover his shame, and blames what he sees – three soldiers, each muddied and blooded as if he has stepped off a battlefield, landing on precisely the same spot, minutes apart – on tricks

35

of his mind. Years later, when he has been persuaded by love that shame is only a story we tell ourselves and are told, and has left the bottle behind, does he remember that day in Waterloo Station. There is someone he tries to tell, but his friend, the chosen confidante, doesn't listen well, not having recovered from the time he appeared in Covent Garden, almost knocking over a flower stall. (He, this one, never tells anyone, never returns to his family, his girl, the Yorkshire town where he grew up. He stumbles through life, a half-remembered smoking child tapping on his frontal lobe, wishing more than once that he had not survived, finding no point in anything at all.)

While we were taking that small detour to London, our girl, our nicotine-addicted child, has sent several more out of battle. She is practised, it becomes faster and faster. Let us slip back inside her mind. Is she really so young, so innocent? Here, an image: she is swaddled and left to cry. Here, another: all skirts and snarling. Our girl is a beast, a she-wolf. Cigarettes are the least of her vices. ("What do you know?" she says. "Tell us." "How to tell," she says, lighting up. "How to tell with only words, images. Leave me alone." "Are you doing this for kindness?" She raps on the card table with her pretty fist. "Kindness? That's not for me to say. Now go.")

At last, there are only two left, two dizzied, half-inhuman soldiers, one of ours, one of theirs. During a sudden silence, they see her, between them, calm at her card table, stubbing ash into the sand. She nods to both.

"Play," she says, and hands them pieces.

"No," says one. (Is he ours? Theirs?) He is half-inhuman, yes, but has enough of him intact to understand that this is a hallucination, it must be. *Mother*, he thinks. "I am dead," he says, not to the girl but to his opposite number, or comrade, or stranger, or intimate, whose eyes are beginning to shade. "We are dead now. It is over."

"No!" says the child, for the first time standing up. She is tiny but she fills the space entirely. "No, you're not. And you will not be from my hands. But you must play."

"Why?" says the second soldier, who finds he speaks their language perfectly. "Why should I not just…" and he sinks to the ground and lies himself down beside the card table. The first soldier, grinning, moves across to lie beside him.

The girl is raging. "No, no no!" she screams, louder than any shell, lighting cigarettes, one, then another, then another, and dropping them so small fires flame. "Don't you see, the game is not finished. The game is not…" (Ah, she has dropped the drawbridge, we are inside her head now, and we see beatings, confinement, all the evil done to children done to this one child, whose heart is grey and strained.)

But the soldiers, one clutching in his hand the top hat, one the iron, will not be moved.

Several centuries pass without a word. The soldiers, peaceful, sleep, their chests expanding, contracting. Our smoking girl quits, then begins again, then quits, counting sand grains to amuse herself. (In Mayfair, down Bond Street, near Marylebone Station, travellers pass through, pass through and on and on.)

Without the game finishing, no more wars can start. The girl knows she has failed in what she was charged to do by those who hired her. Sand sticks under her nails and on her cheeks when, finally, she begins to cry. She cries for all of us. These are tears she was never meant to shed.

The soldiers sleep on, the smoking girl, who has quit her cigarettes, cries, and in Covent Garden, on a flower stall, a man sells a bunch of daffodils, yellower than he has ever sold before, to a woman rushing home, a woman in love, a woman love has taken, for now at least, out of time itself.

The Special Advisor

You did not apply for this job. You applied for another job, but they are offering you this one. You can't imagine that they would ever have advertised this job, though it is described simply enough. They do not give you time to think. You take it. At home later, over dinner warmed from a can, you wonder what skills you possess that made them choose you. You decide that it is probably best not to ask.

This is what they have said you are to do. *When there is a summary execution*, they said, *anywhere in the world, you tell us what you think. You advise.*

Alright, you said.

The first day, there are no summary executions.

You do not have to track them down yourself; there is a staff to do that. You attempt to make conversation with one of them. *Hello*, you say. She does not turn away from her screen.

The remainder of the first week, there are also no summary executions. You explore the building. You locate the fifth floor's kitchen, toilets, smoking balcony. You make coffee. You tidy your desk. You ask for stationery. Rubber bands. Paper clips. You make more coffee.

You receive your door plate. *Special Advisor*, it says, on *Summary Executions*. You wonder what you will tell your mother. This is not a title she can use to boast to her friends. My son the... You do not call her.

You meet another Special Advisor on the Monday morning of your second week. He is advising on something else. *Every now and then, we'll overlap,* he says without going into details. *You are the only one on Summary Executions,* he tells you, as he stirs sugar into his coffee. You really want to ask what happened to the previous advisor, but you are somehow afraid. You tell yourself that this is foolish, that it is not as if he or she might have been...

You smile. You want to appear pleasant, approachable. You feel that with your job title you will have to make an effort. With your job title there might be assumptions.

At last: an execution! In a lawless country known for these things. You are provided with an outline of events; you must do research. *A quick memo within twelve hours,* your friend the other Special Advisor tells you, eating a chocolate digestive. *Then a more detailed reported within twenty-four.* You thank him. You take your coffee and start to scour the online news sources. You find out how old the victim was, how many children he had. You find out that he had been in hiding after numerous incarcerations. That he was beheaded. You read that he was a poet. You look at a picture of him. You enlarge it and stare into his eyes for too long. You get up and pour more coffee.

That night, you order pizza and as you ask for extra mushrooms you imagine a large man with a large knife. When the pizza comes, you remove the mushrooms.

Your brief memo appears to have been sufficient enough not to warrant a response. Your boss' secretary smiles at you and you take this to be a good sign. You work on your longer report. You include translations of some of the victim's poems. You are pleased with this. You describe all the details you have found on the manner of the execution: the type of blade, where and how it has been manufactured throughout history. You are pleased with this, too. You insert the names of the murdered man's children, their ages. You give advice, with wording lifted from the directives you have been given.

Unstable nation...

no indication of pattern...

strongly-worded condemnation...

keeping a watchful eye..

You send the document to print but then you find it difficult to stand up and walk over to the printer. Your knees are uncooperative. It takes more than fifteen minutes.

In bed that night, you see the man's eyes. A line from one of his poems, *Never done and we are never done,* rings through your dreams.

You happen to read an article about octopuses. *They are very intelligent,* you say to your friend the other Special Advisor as you pour coffee. You tell him the story about the octopus whose brain the scientists were trying to research. *They put him to sleep, inserted a probe,* you say, *and the octopus just pulled it out. Really?* says the other Special Advisor. *Just pulled it out?*

Wow! Yes, you say. Then he asks if you'd like to have dinner sometime. You are surprised but you agree. Special Advisors should stick together, you think, as you look for a biscuit.

That night you have a date. Friends fixed you up with her. You are wary. You are nervous. She is a financial analyst. When she smiles and says, *So, what do you do?* you gulp wine, and then you tell her. Soon after, she goes to the bathroom. Soon after that, there is an emergency phone call, *she simply must...* and soon after that, you are alone with half a bottle of house red.

You finish it. You think of the octopus. You imagine his tentacle, gripping the wine bottle, pouring himself a glass. You are grinning to yourself as you pay the bill and walk out into the rain.

There is another one. The information is on your desk. An underworld kingpin, it seems. There is a picture of the kingpin's body. You understand for the first time the phrase *riddled with bullets*. You enlarge the picture but you cannot see his eyes. He has a wife. He has children. He doesn't write poetry. Another country in which *such executions are the norm* although *not a frequent occurrence*. You write your brief memo. You work on your report.

Your friend the other Special Advisor has chosen the restaurant. You meet him there. You are surprised when he orders wine without asking you. You did not do this the other night, with the failed date. You would not presume. But it is good wine. Very good wine. *Tell me more about cephalopods*, says your friend. He leans in closer and you tell him what you remember: how an octopus has been known to carry a large shell around with him or her all day in case, at some point, shelter is needed. *Forward planning*, grins your friend.

Later, after several bottles of the excellent wine, your new friend the other Special Advisor puts his hand over yours. Shock is not the right word to describe your reaction. You cannot move your arm. You don't know where to look. *It's okay*, says your friend. *No rush*. He withdraws his hand. Pays the bill.

There are no more summary executions for the rest of the week. You do some general research. You wander around the building. You occasionally bump into your friend the other Special Advisor in the coffee room. You are not as embarrassed as you thought you would be.

On Friday morning, you sit at your desk, close your eyes, and wonder if octopuses kill. Yes, for food, but each other? You try and picture an octopus wrapping all its tentacles around its enemy. And squeezing. It doesn't feel right. Your imaginary octopus lets go.

Later that day, your friend the other Special Advisor comes to your cubicle. *I have a surprise*, he says. He hands you a biscuit and tells you he will pick you up tomorrow. He won't reveal any more.

65 million years ago, says the researcher, standing in front of her tanks. You are staring at the octopus. The octopus might be staring at you, you aren't sure. *That's when their brains really started to develop*, she says. Your friend the other Special Advisor asks more questions and you hear them talk about nautiluses. You hear the researcher describe one of her octopuses who, if the light in his tank is left on at night, will short-circuit it. You smile at this octopus. You move your hand in an almost-wave. One of the octopus' tentacles moves too. It may just be coincidence.

You turn to your friend. You touch his elbow. You smile.

That night is the first time you go to bed together. He just holds you. You have never been held like this. You listen to him breathe. You feel his heart pumping into you. You slowly slide your hands underneath his chest until it is as if you are just one four-armed and four-legged Special Advisor, holding on and on.

There is another execution. Three women. All have children. None are poets. But none are warriors either. You find their pictures, you look at their faces, you put the pictures under a pile on your desk, you get the pictures out from under the pile, you look at their faces again.

You try to get up and go for coffee. Your knees are unobliging. It takes over fifteen minutes. The other Special Advisor, who is now more than a friend, pours for you, says nothing, hands you chocolate digestives. When the others finally leave the kitchen, the other Special Advisor puts a hand on

your shoulder. You take the coffee and the chocolate digestives back to your desk but when your hand moves towards
the pictures of the three women, the shaking returns.

When you are in bed together, you and your lover, the other
Special Advisor, do not talk about work. You compete with
each other to unearth the funniest news items, the oddest
things humans are doing. Siamese twins who make their fortunes from online trading. A two-year-old girl who has composed twelve symphonies. A space umbrella designed to shift
rainstorms. There is rarely a time when you do not both have
something fantastical to share, and when you have laughed,
when you have made love – which you are astonished to find
never makes you uncomfortable, inhibited, shy – you sometimes jointly wonder at the world in which this can be so.
Where is the normal? you ask each other. *Where is the still?*

After a month, you are summoned for review. Your boss
tells you that they are impressed with your thoroughness.
Your boss begins to say something about your predecessor
but stops himself. He looks towards the large windows of
his office and out over the city. Then your boss turns back
to you, a false smile on his face. He thanks you again, sees
*no need for further review until the completion of the three month
probationary period.* You understand that you are doing well.

You had questions. You had the words of a poem under your tongue. You had many pairs of eyes inside your
head, looking out through your eyes towards your boss as

45

if he held answers. As you reach your desk, you hold on to your chair and take a long deep breath. Then you move your computer mouse and watch the screensaver disintegrate.

There is a morning where you wake up and decide not to go to work. You do not call your boss. You do not call your lover, who has not spent the night because of working late. You do not phone anyone.

You leave your home and stand out in the street a while. You turn right and that is when you choose where you will go.

The researcher is surprised but friendly. The octopus does not seem surprised. You sit by the octopus's tank with the cup of tea the researcher made for you. You wonder about the octopus. You wonder if the octopus wonders about you. You try not to think of the poet, the kingpin, the three mothers.

You and the octopus have been there for several hours when you hear someone else come round the tanks towards you. You expect the researcher. Or perhaps your lover, worrying about you. But you do not know the woman. She is not wearing a lab coat. She looks at you as if you are who she has come to see. She does not look at the octopus.

I think we should talk, she says. *I think you want to meet me.*

You are confused. Is she an expert in cephalopods? Had you mentioned you wanted to learn more?

And then, as if you are slapped hard, you know exactly who she is.

*You...,*you say. *You are my...You did my...*

She blinks twice, clears her throat. She looks away and then she looks right at you. *You see their faces,* she says. *You hear them. Their eyes are in you. They look out through your eyes. You have trouble with your knees. You find it hard to get out of the chair.*

Yes, you whisper. You can't look at her because she sees too much of you, so you stare at the octopus. Your chest is filled with something liquid. Your heart is swimming. Nothing is said out loud at all.

And then you open your mouth. And then you say: *I see them all the time I hear them I feel like they are watching me he wrote poems the body was full of holes they all had children so many children I don't understand how someone can how someone does what did they do the mothers the others he was just a poet well maybe one of them was criminal but the women the women they whisper in my ear how is it that one person can do and to another and what if I could what if we could what if it's just pretending not to what if underneath the suits I go into the coffee room and everyone's polite and on my desk on my desk there is this pile there are pictures and they stare at me and then my legs don't work my knees don't work I can't slice food without thinking and is this going on and it just comes at me comes at me why is it coming at me as if they are doing it for me doing it to me for me his eyes his poems I can't I can't I can't.*

and when you are gasping too much to carry on you feel a chaos and you turn and the octopus is thrashing, whirling round its tank, tentacles whacking and slashing at the walls, at each other, at the octopus's head and your heart is paddling as you bend towards the tank, as you whisper *Shhhh, shhh*. Your new friend, the former Special Advisor, kneels down too and you both put your palms onto the tank's cool glass, you press your cheek there, and right then you cannot remember who is in the tank and who is outside. The octopus begins to slow down, its tentacles sliding around the tank, slipping towards its floor. Through your cheek you feel the violence as it ebbs away.

You hear voices and two researchers wander into your section of the lab. When they see you, they giggle and stare. Your new friend lifts herself up and then she holds out her hand to you. You let her pull you to standing then you lean on the top of the tank, your body still unsolid.

Sorry, you say. *Don't be*, she says.

You leave the lab together. You take the lift down and then you are in the street, facing one another. You do not know how this will end. You have no idea how this will end.

Then she says what she says to you and, like another slap, you know it all.

You don't have to, she says, and walks away.

You watch her reach the end of the street, then vanish. You think of open landscapes, of the sea filled with every type of life. You breathe in. You breathe out. Your heart is sad but still. Your heart is you. You think about your mother. You realise it has been a long long time. You turn and walk the other way, thinking of what you will tell her about your day.

A Scar Sits Above My Heart

On our muffled furniture, sofa straining under covers, we sit, my hand in your hand, her hand and his hand, and we watch the silent tick of snow on television screen, yet to be hooked in. Our thighs strain to the stillness, your hand in my hand, his and hers legs and arms and breathing, soft and long under the snow's cold fizzing. We welcome injury or collision to throw us from the seat, to fling us to the floor and leave us scarred. A scar, reminder of you on me, you burning, me deflating, sits above my heart. I slip my hand from yours, he sits, she stands, the television hushes, outside simple streets swing past.

Telling Time

Stopwatching
And What If All Your Blood Ran Cold
Empty But For Darwin
The Plan or You Must Remember This
Tunnelling

"I'm tailor-made for timings, she not so much".

Stopwatching

I'm tailor-made for timings, she not so much, and so she stands and does the slowness, the almost-creeping still things, and I do the rushings-around, the speedings and flashings-past. It keeps me up and up, I don't tire, I have the limbs and eyes for tracking, even tachyons, no matter speeds of light, of heat, of black, of white or pink or yellow or life or death. I'm thinking beyond death and space and planets, while she, nearly non-breathing, takes care of stasis.

She comes to me, slowly, slowly, once, and tells me, slowly, slowly, all her cares, how her anxiety is more intense than ever, and I glance at her in between my timings, take her in part by part, not understanding what this means, as limes and roses blow between us. I want to question but I don't know the glass of her language, fear my words will burn her with acceleration, so I say nothing and she slinks away.

But as I stopwatch, as I record the darts and dashings, I can't help but notice her gone-ness, where is she now, where does she stand in the trapezoid of toasts and raisings of glasses and smashings of our existence? I slip and trip around to find her but she escapes me, and when Night unhoods I wonder if I might unspeed myself, develocitize. I self-brake and self-brake and when I am at such tardies that I have never tried, there she is.

At these scales and sizes she almost rushes me, she almost swamps me and she's limes and roses blowing and she's all of time and not of time and when she reaches up to me and I reach up to her, there in a moment, minute, parsec, light second, we are still: frozen but not cold, frozen but not dead or dying, frozen there together, smiling.

And What If All Your Blood Ran Cold

We do it gradually. Well, you have to, don't you. No
replacing all someone's blood in a hurry. We've not
done it on a real patient, you have to wait, for the
right kind to turn up. Exactly the precise situation
where this might work. Which doesn't happen often. The patient who has no other chance, who is going to die. Who *is* going to die. That kind of patient.

There's someone here whose job it is to keep track.
Of how many do die. Our mortality rates. She sits at her
desk, she has a spreadsheet. She is excellent with those.
She loves numbers, lists, moving and shuffling them
around. But every now and then she comes down, stands
in a corner and watches. I see her there, like a ghost, as
we're resuscitating, intubating, all the blood, the noise.
She hovers there in her corner and there's a look on
her face, I see it as I rush past. I can't place that look.

She's in love. No, not with me. I don't know who
with. Not yet. But she sits at her desk, and although she's
precise, she has files and folders keeping track of heart
attacks, infections, of treatments given, of the names of
those who fill the morgue, the cold ones whose hearts
we weren't meant to restart, whose infections resisted all
our efforts, she's not focussed. Not anymore. She used to
be. When she first arrived, she was keen as mustard. She
didn't come down to watch then. She was all about figures.

Maybe it's not love, maybe it's death. Or deaths.
All of it. But I'm pretty sure. Because being surrounded by the almost-dying is what you get used to
here. It's not what begins to slide under your skin; it
rolls off. Whatever's eating her, it's something else.

We've only practised it so far, the new technique, on the
newly-dead. With permission, of course. There were no
loved ones then, we used homeless people, people no-one
claimed. Hospital lawyers gave the go-ahead. After all,
it's to save lives, no? And they were already. Unsaveable.

She wasn't there then. No-one watched because
we were clumsy, slow, we bungled. It's a lot of work,
the wholesale blood removal. It's a lot of liquid.
Hours. It's not like we dry them out - we replace the
blood. With salt water. It's cooler, the body tem-
perature drops and then they can stay like that while
we try and fix them. That's the theory, anyway.

I think the person she's in love with, our death account-
ant, isn't someone she works with. She's not got that silly,
I've-just-seen-my-beloved look when she watches us.

It's cold. So
cold. They
think I don't
know. They
think I can't. But
I do. I
am. Still.

You know, I'm not the only one, there's one of me in every hospital. Accountants of doom, that's what we call ourselves, our joke, when we get together! It's not like we're doing the killing, we say, and we do laugh about it because if you don't laugh about it, when you do what we do, what else happens but that you go home every night, every night, and sit and look at the moon and drink something to stop yourself from thinking about it but then you dream about it anyway, all the ways. You soak it into yourself when you are the one who knows all the dead, all the dying, it's inside your skin, and you've got no barrier, no anti-morbid raincoat, which is something else we laugh about. What a gap in the market! we say as we pass around the Hobnobs. Someone needs to develop that kind of technology, help the doom accountants! Then we giggle, there do seem to be a lot of gigglers among us, no matter what age, no matter how long you've been doing what we do. If you saw me sitting in my office, if you saw me in front of my computer, you might think I was so serious, checking my spreadsheets, with all the different flavours of death in neat columns, with dates, times, of course. But inside I'm probably chuckling at something someone has sent by email, one of those cartoons, Death doing this, someone cheating Death, you know the kind of thing. We laugh a lot. Part of the job gets me out from behind the desk, I have to go and talk to the staff about what the situation is, quite often, I do the rounds, I wander, and I ask quietly, gently, about this week, about the almost-dying,

the almost-died, the chances of, the attempts to save, and
there isn't much laughing then, of course, we're usually
in the corridors, I don't like to take too much of their
time. They're the ones doing the saving, the resuscitating,
the caring. I just add it up. I just do the sums. Who's left
us this week, and who gets to stay for a while longer.

We found one! I know, don't sound too excited. But
– the perfect candidate. They tried everything else
on him. Motorbike. Silly bugger. So we snap into action. Not the best coordinated team, despite the practice. I mean, all those years of med school but the
minute you come out and there you are, real world,
it's different. There's no pausing. It's all blood and in-
sides and people crying and, hopefully, patients hugging you and actually leaving the hospital. Properly.
    So we did it. Drained him and refilled. It all seemed
to work. The saline instead of blood. And now
we've got time. Or rather, he's got time. We hope.

It's cold. So
cold. They
think I don't.
They
think I
can't. But
I
do. I
am. Still.

We do talk, when we all get together, about why we ended
up in this job, we know it's not something our parents
can boast about, My Daughter the Death Statistician! We
know that it's a job that's as old as the hills, of course, all
throughout history someone was charged with adding
them up, the fallen. Or someone took it upon themselves,
the Chroniclers. How many died in wars, how many in
fires, plagues, pestilence. We humans, we like numbers,
we find some kind of comfort, maybe from the fact –
we discussed this last time we met – that because we're
reading the numbers it means we're not one of them,
we're not on The List, not yet, and we can pretend we
never will be. Or it's some kind of talisman, you know:
talk about it, read about it, do the sums, but me, never,
I'm immortal! We know better than anyone about
immortality. We know better than anyone the chances.
They're greater now – clean hands, antibiotics, surgical
techniques, robots, nanoparticles, on and on. But still,
the viruses get smarter and shiftier, who knows what's
in the air around my desk, or what's coming in through
that window? You just don't. You just never know.

And while we're working on him, Bike Boy, she comes
down. She stands for a while in the corner of the room,
and then she says, to all of us, What's happening exactly?
And I see my chance, so I tell her. Replacing his blood?
she says. All of it? Yes, I say, and she says, So he's still…

alive? Without… blood? Ah, I say, well, that's sort of
tricky. Tricky? she says, and she tilts her head to one side
and I swear she's almost grinning. He's in a sort of…
I say. Suspended animation, I think that's the technical
term, and here her eyes light up, honestly. Oh my god,
she says, and her hands do this fluttering thing. I don't
have a column for that, I don't have…Neither do we!
I say, and for a moment we're both standing and grinning at each other. Then I'm called back and before I
turn around she says, How long…? and I say, Well, it's
experimental, you know. We just don't. We really…

    I want to tell everyone, I want to email round and say,
    Guess what, I had to create a new category, I've got a
    new column, do you know about this, suspended, half-
    way-between? But of course, I can't, it's experimental, it's
    hush hush, it's more than that, hush hush hush HUSH.
    My fingers are itching to do it, but instead I choose a
    new colour for the category, I write his name down,
    a tick in that column. For now. And then I sit, and I
    think I'm sitting for ages and ages, wondering about it,
    wondering if he knows, wondering, for the first time
    really, you'd think I'd thought more about how dead
    might feel, but this is someone who might feel it and then
    come back. Come back. Jesus, Mary, Joseph, and all the
    others, this really does feel like some sort of witchcraft.

They worked on him, Bike Boy, for days. That's the point of all of this: time. Time, the thing we run out of round here, the main element which we wish we could bag and attach like a drip. Slow it all down, as we run and run, we're running to try and outrun it. So this, if it works... my god. I mean, last night I sat at home and thought, What if we could do this with everyone who comes in? Slip in a drain, slide out all your blood, salt and cool you, and then we'd be walking, dancing, as we fixed you up, no? We could say, Oh look at that liver, hmm, what should we do? And then we'd sit and drink tea, weigh up our options. And you'd be oh so chilled. And then I thought, But we don't know anything about what'd be in your head. Would you be having dreams of walking through Antarctica, being trapped inside a freezer, becoming icicles? And then I thought of her, and I remembered how we'd grinned at each other, her and me, at this new thing, this new category. Newness. Isn't always better, though, is it?

When the time came, or rather, when the point arrived after which no-one knew what might happen to Bike Boy in his suspension, I thought she might like to see it, so I went upstairs to find her. She was at her desk and, before she saw me, I watched her. It's rare to see someone doing what she does looking so damn happy. Even gleeful. I mean, she's a numbers person, she's not reaching into chests to start a heart, she's not inventing things, she's not teaching, and I know that all sounds patronising as hell, but it's true, no? I tapped on the glass. When she turned, first she looked wor-

ried, but I grinned, to help. And realised how I'd wanted her
to look at me like she'd looked at her screen, her lists. Happy.

We stood around his bed, so many of us, me the only
one, I guess, not really a medical person, it was so nice of
them to let me, to send someone to come and fetch me for
this. I was trying not to seem as excited as I was feeling.
My god! Here was this guy, in suspended animation,
hovering, hovering in my brand new category, and we –
they – were about to bring him back. And you could feel
it, a wave shivering between all of us, I've never known
anticipation like that, so thick, like we could pass it round,
a rope of it tying us together. It was simple: they'd done
all the hooking up, someone nodded at someone, who
pressed a button, there was whirring, and we all stared
at his face. His face! The blood was coming back into
him, I couldn't see where exactly. His blood, that they'd
kept. Nudging all the saline out the way, and it made me
think of some cartoon, of little blood men arriving and
the salt maidens not wanting to leave, and I did have to
stop myself giggling because this was serious, this was
it, this was the moment. A sort of miracle, perhaps.

She was watching Bike Boy's face, so was everyone, we
were all pretending we weren't unbelievably desperate for
it, for it to have worked. But I was watching her. That
might sound like I'm in love with her or something, but
I'm not, I don't have it in me, not for love, not right now.

Something about her makes me so curious, about her
job, how she goes on when she's staring at it every day.
She's staring at it not in the way we do, she can't think,
Death, how can I try and avoid it, how can I save this
one? She must be thinking, One death, and another one,
and another one… and on and on. How does she do it?

Nothing happened, and more nothing happened, and it
wasn't like those films, where when they zoom into a close
up of the coma person's face and you know that their
eyelids are going to do that twitchetty thing and someone
will come running and shouting, She's awake! Real life
doesn't work on a schedule that suits an audience. We
stood there and then after about 20 minutes there was
some more nodding and someone said, Well, it might
take a while, and we all began to wander off and I went
back upstairs to stare at my categories. I put my mouse
over his name, I highlighted it as if I was going to move
it, from its own special hush hush column into one. Or
the other. And I really felt, really truly and so strongly,
that if I moved him, it might… I might be able to. And
I swear, I started shaking. I dropped my mouse and I put
my hand over my own heart and it was like a drum was
inside me, someone was pounding on it, just pounding.

Later, I went and stood by him. Nothing. Nothing had
changed. He was officially, medically, himself again, I
mean, he was all blood, no salt. But he hadn't moved, no

twitching, no sighing, nothing. He was still on the ventilator, we were doing all his functions for him. I bent down. I bent down right by his ear as if I was going to whisper something. But I didn't know. I just didn't know what to say and I felt like a right idiot, so I fiddled, made it look like I was just checking. And when I got up, she was there.

"Nothing?"
"Nothing. Nope."
"How much longer? I mean…"
"No-one knows. We've really got no clue, this is so…"

<table>
<tr><td>We stood there</td><td>We stood there</td></tr>
<tr><td>The two of us</td><td>The two of us</td></tr>
<tr><td>And then, suddenly</td><td>Suddenly.</td></tr>
<tr><td>It wasn't just</td><td>the two of us anymore.</td></tr>
<tr><td>Suddenly</td><td>Suddenly</td></tr>
</table>

there were three.

Empty But For Darwin

The pawn was being tricksy. Pawns were always difficult but this one kept slipping from his fingers. He put down the brush, took another sip of scotch. At least it was only one colour. He'd had much fiddlier requests: the whole set striped – or once even done with dots like those artists did, the pointillists, he thinks they're called. His eyes wouldn't manage that now, would they, little pawn? He picked it up again, took the brush between his teeth. Oh come on, stop being waffly, it's only a job it's not a masterpiece. He'd given up all thoughts of masterpieces years before, after she'd gone. Now he just painted knights and kings and queens and lots of tricksy pawns.

In a garden, there was science. That was the intention anyway, the Designers had their brief. The garden didn't understand. Would it be required to experiment? Would it be necessary to repeat and repeat and repeat? Or keep coming up with unanswered questions about the universe? The trees were puzzled, why a science garden? Why not just let us be. But the Designers were being paid for this and this would be a First.

The knight was fine once you got your fingers at the right angle, held it up, swivelled it around. He was running out of whisky now and his eyes were sore. He put the knight back with his naked compatriots and enemies, and lay down on his sofa. There was not much light left, and he didn't like to work with artificial, the buzzing of the lamps. Aren't you a sensitive damn thing, he told himself. First tricksy pawns and now noise. At his age... oh now, at *my* age, goodness, when did *I* become so tricksy? And he missed her more and more right then because that was her voice in his head, his little Queen who'd so long ago now disappeared. My board is empty without you, he told her.

The first science was Biology. The Designers were given a list of words, that started small (cell and spine and eye and DNA and RNA) and became longer (flagella, intestine, lymphocyte, keratinase). They sat in the garden, the trees peering over the Designers' shoulders, trying to decide what to do with all this vocabulary. We can have words! shouted one Designer, older than the rest, more traditional, more experienced. No words, it's all about the plants! the Lady Designer shrieked. She stood up and although she was tiny against the Old Designer's bulk, he wobbled and fell back onto the grass. The Handsome Young Designer said nothing, dreaming of rhododendrons, cacti, trailing ivy.

He took the set along to the shop when it was dry. He'd had a terrible time with the pawns, drunk much more than usual just to get it finished. His fingers wouldn't do it anymore. At some point, faint and dizzy, he'd heard the pieces taunting him and it was all he could do to stop himself from beheading every single one. Shut the fuck up, he'd mumbled, sinking into the sofa. Come back, my Queen, come back, it's just a game. You know that. The shop owner didn't look too closely, the work was always good, just handed over cash. Half he put deep in his bag and went down to his local. A pattern, never changing. Just getting more ingrained.

The Designers were working on the section modelled on A Brain. You have to have one to know one, grumbled the Old Designer, knowing the Lady was behind him. She contemplated shoving him but didn't want to injure flora. She was modelling a vine into neuronal connections while the Young Designer she had eyes for was immersed in contemplating dendrites. Using them to create them! she had joked to him but he had just turned his pale blue eyes on her and hadn't smiled. She stood for a moment and wondered about the blood-brain barrier. Can it really not be penetrated or was their info out of date? She thought of a red flowing stream, but how to dye it? The Young Designer bent a willow back and forth and the Lady watched the muscles in his forearm flex and mould.

He didn't have a new commission and, quite glad, he sat at the bar and thought of his week ahead. Time for a quick game? With all the painting he hadn't had the chance to play. Sipping his Laphroaig, he traced his way mentally through his flat to find the board that started it all. Probably in the cupboard he hadn't touched after she died. Well, one of many. He took a bigger slug of whisky, turned to the barman who was waiting with the bottle. Nice to be known, he thought, even if I am predictable.

In the garden, they'd moved on to Physics, no less a mystery to the Designers than Biology. Some words they found familiar – We can do Energy! they cried. We can do Light! – but a neutrino, quark or solenoid? What is relativity? Gravity is manageable, but we don't know about particle colliders made of plants. How about a bust of Einstein made of water lilies? said the Handsome Young Designer, and the Lady clapped her hands. But the Old Designer grouched and muttered, What happens when it rains, be just like he's crying, that won't do, he skuffled. But he was overruled and they began to create Albert's visage while the Old Designer scattered daisies angrily to mimic quantum leaps.

He played both himself and his opponent, something he used to do when no-one else was around. When she wasn't there to challenge him. The set was beautiful, each piece a different scientist, he'd made them just for her: Marie and Pierre Curie, Faraday, there's Crick and Watson. She'd supplied the pictures, and his young fingers had no problems then. The Curies were black King and Queen, not that they were evil, she told him, how were they to know? But it seemed wrong to make them white. Albert Einstein was a knight, riding off to new horizons, on a light ray, she'd said as she explained about his theories. Now, as he played the game, he remembered how he hadn't really taken in anything at all, except her neck, her cheeks, her earlobes. You aren't going to quiz me, are you? he had teased, but she kept on and on, even as he kissed her, talking Newton, Darwin, Edison.

The Designers faced their biggest challenge yet. I don't understand these equations, moaned the Lady. Prime numbers, said the Handsome Young Designer with a grimace. What is it, asked the Old Designer, failing to imagine anything. They sat as the sun went down, passing flowers to each other, round and round, and still nothing came. When it got dark, the Old Designer stumbled to the gate, and left the Lady and the Handsome one alone. I see it, I'm not stupid, he whispered as he held onto an oak tree to catch his breath.

He had to leave the house. He'd received an order but his fingers wouldn't do it. No matter how much whisky - or how little. He had to take the pieces back, unpainted. He felt quite sick, mostly because of drink; he knew how stupid he was being. Doesn't matter does it, he thought, as he stared at the pond and realised what the water lilies made. Hello, he said, and fished the piece out of his pocket. Albert, meet Albert. And he tossed it in the water. He felt a wave of rightness, which immediately subsided. To bring it back, he buried Pierre and Marie underneath the X-Ray bush, and slipped Newton into the branches of the Gravi-tree.

When his pockets were empty but for Darwin, he lay down on the grass. An old man walked past, grumbling. Behind him he could hear two people whisper, then a woman's giggle. I'm evolving, Charles, he told the piece. Then he closed his eyes and let maths, physics and biology do their thing.

The Plan or You Must Remember This

10.

Look at the Memory Man run! There he goes! We knew he'd run. We didn't know when exactly or in which direction, but we knew. Doors were left slightly ajar, locks not quite locked. Yes, we're recording it, we're videoing him. Of course we are, for later analysis – of his speed, direction, gait, the prevailing wind. Go, Memory Man, go! How will he remember this? We won't be able to ask him, not this time. Look at him, you've got to be impressed with it all, at his age. His knees look quite stiff, oops, he's stumbled. But Memory Man picks himself straight up, not even looking behind to see if we're following. Of course we're not following. That would defeat the purpose. He has to go. It's his time to go now. Farewell, Memory Man, we'll see you soon. We hope we've left you with... well, if not happy, then at least new. Memories. Ones you won't... Well, you don't, do you? Forget.

9.

He sits quite still now, he doesn't fidget like he did at first. He knows. We know. We all know. He is our Memory Man, we have him. For the moment, anyway. We are in no doubt as to his skills. And we are in no doubt how we can use his skills. Imagine if we had to train someone to be like him instead? Imagine how long that would take! We can't imagine it, we sit around in the evenings, with our beers and we laugh at how we might have had to contemplate, to work up a schedule, to fiddle with the subject, fiddle being used here purely technically, ha ha! We think we could have done it, we have faith in our skills, we're highly trained ourselves of course. But the paperwork to fill in for permission, we yawn at that, we raise our arms high, we slap wrists and palms. Our Memory Man saved us so much form-filling, thank you Memory Man, are we glad we found you!

8.
Our second Day Out is a success, we decide. Memory Man performs well, "above expectations" we will write later on the evaluation. We take him to more complex locations, "greater association of variables" we will write later. We record it all, as per usual, audio, video, thermal, all of that. We are also testing new equipment. Well, he is our new equipment too, ha ha! We are testing the BWM, we will use Memory Man to calibrate it, now we know we can trust him. As far as we can throw him, eh! He's too heavy for that, of course. We did think about some kind of propulsion…No, that was just one of those late-night, beer-tinted ideas, the ones you remember in the morning, hazy, and think, Now why would we even suggest…! Not in the report. That one's been ditched.

7.

He's had a bad day. And when Memory Man has a bad day, we all have a bad day. We understand now, can't ask about the wife. Don't mention the war, ha ha! The weeping was, well, disturbing. Memory Man's hands had to be bandaged, just gently, just for a while, after that. We might not put that in the report. Although when others come to examine our findings, they will understand the adversity. They will understand we're not working with chimps here but people, a real person. Bad days happen. We nearly went in there, thought about a hug, when he went on about her death. But we stay away from dying, not a good idea, taints the objectives, outcomes all messed up, you understand. We do feel bad for him, we all said later that night, with our beers. Imagine never forgetting that. Imagine it always being right there, in your head. And we had a minute's quiet, all of us thinking of the thing we wouldn't want to remember the way Memory Man can, in all its detail, vivid like this morning. Then we shook our heads, opened another beer.

6.

He doesn't mind the MRI machine. We were concerned, some people hate small spaces, the banging noises, all that. And if Memory Man had been one of them, we would have been sunk. Truly Titanic. But he's calm as we slide him in, calm as he's always been, helped along of course by a little... That won't go in the report, of course. But after we discovered, through some trial and error, that it didn't impair his abilities, we now use it without a second thought. Once he's in and it's all turned on, we're peachy, good to go. We ask some of the same questions, check against previous answers, he's spot on, exactly. We're still a little freaked out by how he does this. Then we ask new ones, based on his time with us as well as a few more world events thrown in there. And we watch what happens in Memory Man's brain. It's fascinating. Really. Our paper will be... Okay, fine, we mustn't get ahead of ourselves. Still a ways to go.

5.

We have several almanacs to hand, and the online data, of course, to cross check. He gets a little irritated after a while, "subject tired, three hours perhaps too much" we will write in our evaluation. Memory Man, which is what we call him in our writing, it has to be anonymous, of course, keeps asking why all the focus on elections. Ha ha, we say, we're trying to predict the next one! It's a joke, but he doesn't seem to find it funny. He gives all the right answers, who was voted in and where and when, down to the hour sometimes, it's really quite amazing. We're in awe, we say over beer in the evening, in the common room. Awe, literally, we say, and then we try and test our own memories. Can't remember what we had for breakfast, and we laugh! He's truly exceptional, our Memory Man. Truly.

4.

Today's the day! He arrives on time, we had been worried, of course. He didn't have to come, did he? We may have explained it all, national security, finger to nose and all that, it's for your country. But still, how many citizens are civic-minded these days? It's a dying trait, love for one's country, patriotism, hijacked by the loonies. Loonies in the technical sense, of course, ha ha! He looks nervous, which is normal, we're a group, we have each other, he's just him. Alone. No spouse, children, not many friends, real friends, which is use-ful, frankly, for our purposes, although we don't say so. Not in our report. We make him tea, we make a fuss of him, we make a show as if we're telling him everything he needs to know, although of course that would be impossible. We see his breathing slow, his pupils alter, he's trusting us now. Phew, we say later over beers. It could have gone bad from the start! But he settles in, tells us to hit him with whatever we've got, he can handle it! That's quite funny, really, given what we... We laugh about that later too. "Hit him," we say, ha ha!

3.

We like pubs. In objective terms, of course. Generally speak-ing. They contain such a wealth of material, behaviours, con-versational traits. We couldn't model these artificially, they're chaos at its best. And the range of beverages and snacks helps too, ha ha! We spot him quite quickly, the photograph ob-tained is fairly accurate. We zoom in, note down what he's drinking, how he sits, but the most important is audio, of course. He doesn't begin right away. They ease into it, some jokes, although we can see he's not the funny man, he's not the comedian, it's stilted. He has his thing and it's not humour. When they start, we look at each other and we are impressed. Mightily. Whatever they come up with, he can answer. His memory is incredible! We wonder if he's faking it, of course. But he doesn't know that we're… observing. This is his usual, this is Monday night down the Dog and Duck. There's money involved, small wagers we observe. But it's not about that. Not really. It's pride. We see it on his face. This is his Thing. The rest of his life, we know, is not fulfilling in any way. Monday nights are what keeps him going.

2.

We review the reports at lunchtime, over Wednesday pasta salad. There are several possibilities, we are delighted, there is enough to begin at least. Two women, one man, all in middle age, spread around the country. Both women are married, several children, active lives, which makes it a little tricky. They would be missed, we chuckle over cold pasta. But the man, he lives alone. He could be the one. We decide he will be our first, might be the only, who knows how many of them there are? This is new to us. But the fact that we found three is promising. We didn't know if we'd find any at all, it was a hypothesis, something we threw out there, made it sound plausible enough for funding. We high five each other in the cafeteria. Then we go back to the lab and work on our protocol.

1.

It's always defects, we tell our boss. We study what doesn't work well, but what about if it works really really well? Our boss looks intrigued so we press on. Super-memory, we say. We've heard of it, just rumours. Think of what we could… We don't need to finish our sentence, our boss is nodding, agreeing, signing our funding application. Yes! we say when we are out of his office. Then we are a little sheepish because really, it's just rumours, we don't know if we'll find anything, anyone. We make our plans, get in touch with our investigators, send them out with vague instructions. We hope. That's what we have right now. Hope.

Tunnelling

You scramble forward and pretend not to see but how not to see? He sees you not seeing and he lifts it higher. He is on his knees. You are like an animal. A squirrel in the trees is watching. Shouting. And it's you. The squirrel starts and slips and you stop and he drops it and all three of you are frozen then and there, and there is where you're found, afterwards. So long afterwards that you – are you still you? – are only bones and he is only bones. And the squirrel? Only dust.

Now, you and he float above and watch the finding of you, watch them scrabble and unearth, under mounds and under years. He is still trying to show you something as you shimmer in your cloud. And you are still pretending not to see. The squirrel speaks. It is no surprise. Earth, sun and moon, we forget, are spirits too.

All Talk

Empty Too
The Perfect Egg
A Call to Arms
All Activity is Silent

"Imagine," he said softly, 'if they did war that way too.'"

Empty Too

"Tell me truly," she said to him, "what it is that you want."

"I'm sorry," he said, peering into the empty lunchbox, lunchboxes and emptiness disturbing him greatly.

"You know that this is something," she said, turning her neck from one side to another.

"Gone," he said, sliding his fingers around the inside of the lunchbox as if to find the hidden sandwich, chocolate bar, small box of Sunmaid raisins.

"I've never felt this way," she said, and cracked one knuckle, then another.

"It was here," he said, turning the lunchbox upside down and shaking it.

"I'll be whatever you want me to be," she said, closing one eye and squinting.

"It's never the way you think," he said and felt he might cry.

"Mother, whore, saint," she said, and sat on her hands.

"On television someone would have arrived by now," he said, and tossed the lunchbox into the corner.

"I'd tie myself in knots and drop myself into the ocean for you," she said, and bent her head towards her knees.

He said nothing. He stared at the lunchbox and stared and stared.

She said nothing. She hung her head and felt the vertebrae in her spine twist and elongate. Day turned into afternoon and then night. And they were too.

The Perfect Egg

He looks up and catches its eye. Eye? Silly! Visual circuitry. Optical sensors. But he's sure, he's sure it looked right at him. He eats his perfectly boiled egg. Can't stop himself from saying,

"Thank you, this is just right," and swears he sees pleasure, just a hint, on its flawless face. Then it turns and begins to load the dishwasher. He dunks his toast into the runny yolk and tries not to dwell on it.

When he finishes, he gets up and puts his plate, knife and spoon into the sink. It is standing there, waiting.

"Please clean out the fridge, including the ice trays," he says. "They need defrosting." It nods. Is there a smile? I'm going mad, he thinks. He puts on his coat and leaves.

In the park he watches more of them sitting on benches, watching their charges in the playground. He's struck by what they *don't*. Don't fidget, scratch or mess with their hair. Don't turn their head, chat with one another, read magazines or talk on mobile phones. They are absolutely still, completely focused. Just *there*.

He is tempted to run up and grab a child off the swings, just reach around its waist and pull the small body out, shrieking.

Just to see.

Just to know.

That night, he watches television while it irons in a corner of the living room. He is distracted from the sitcom that he won't admit he waits for each week by the smell of steaming fabric, the handkerchiefs he's had for forty years or more, always neatly pressed. Worn a little, torn, but clean and wrinkle-free.

He stands up, and, over by the ironing board, makes a big show of unzipping his fly.

No stirring. Not a flicker. It stops ironing and waits for further instructions.

He takes the trousers off, one leg and then the other, wobbling slightly as he tries to keep his dignity. He hands them over.

"Please do these too," he says, and sits back on the sofa in his underwear. He starts to laugh as on the screen, the wife comes home and shouts at the useless husband.

Next morning, after another perfect egg with toast, he says, "Come with me". It walks behind him to the hall.

He opens the door to the cupboard underneath the stairs.

"Please go inside," he says, and it obeys. He shuts the door and goes upstairs to his study where for several hours in his head are words like *blackness, suffocation, boredom*.

He switches on the computer and writes a long email to the woman who used to be his wife, rambling and no punctuation. He says things he wished he'd said in life, or in that life, at least. At first he calls it poetry and then he sees it's not. He deletes it and goes back down.

He walks about in the kitchen and from kitchen to living

room, living room to downstairs bathroom. Then he stands in the hall, listening. He opens the cupboard door. Dark, no movement at all. It has no lights on. Oh my god, he thinks.

"Are you…?" he says.

It whirrs quickly out of Sleep mode.

"Please, come out," he says. It glides past him, nothing in its eyes or on its face. He has a sensation in his sinuses, unpleasant, unwelcome. He boils the kettle, leaves the full mug of tea on the counter, gets his coat and leaves.

In the park, he watches them again. Are they watching him watching them watching? He ambles over to the swings and puts a hand out, leaning on the rail as small girls giggle and try to touch the sky. No-one moves or does anything. No-one even looks in his direction.

How fast could they run if…?

Would it be just the one who'd tackle him to the playground floor? Or all of them, some sort of instantaneous communication rousing them to action?

After a few minutes, the screams and creaking of the swings give him shooting pains through his skull. He heads for home.

He eats dinner, listening to the radio, the evening news. He finishes, puts the plate in the sink, then he says:

"Please come with me,"

and leads them both upstairs. In the bedroom he instructs it to sit in the armchair in the corner. He puts on his pyjamas with some coyness, a wardrobe door shielding him. Then he gets into bed and pulls the covers tight around himself.

"Please watch," he tells it. "Just keep an eye. Make sure that nothing... I mean, no sleeping."

He switches off his bedside light and can see a faint green glow coming from the armchair. He lies with his eyes open for a few moments and then he falls asleep.

In the morning, refreshed, he eats his perfect egg.

"Thank you," he says and puts his plate, knife and form into the sink. "Please do the carpets today," he tells it and heads towards the stairs.

A Call To Arms

"15-love," the carer said, and served again. The old man stared hard at the TV screen. The ball came towards him and he willed his arm to move.

"30-love," the carer said.

"Oh dear," said the old man.

"Never mind," she said, and served again.

This time the old man's arm did twitch and wobble, but the ball just sank sadly onto bright green grass.

"40-love," the carer said.

In the third game, the old man finally made contact, satisfying twang of ball on racket. Went into the net.

"Well done!" the cheerful carer said.

"Gosh," the old man said, and brought a hand up to his forehead, wiped it down.

They played til teatime. The carer switched it off and when the giant screen went dark the old man's world turned back to grey and yellow.

"Tennis!" he said. "Well."

"Wonderful!" the cheerful carer said, and wheeled him to the living room.

The old man held his teacup, looked around for someone near. On his left, but that one wasn't much for conversation, she was gone already.

He took a sip and then said loudly:

"Tennis. Just played a game. Still doing it, you know. You can."

No-one spoke. A cough from somewhere, shouting in the corner where some poor soul was being made to eat.

"I did it in my chair," he told the room, which wasn't listening. "Didn't need much else, it's all on telly now. You move your arm and somehow it just knows you've done it."

He stopped for breath, took another sip of tea and reached out for a biscuit.

"Imagine what could be," he said. "I don't mean golf or football. My grandkids, they point their arms and shoot at dragons, rescuing princesses. All that bang-bang."

Bang-bang, and on that screen inside his head it all went muddy red and brown and he was there again.

"Imagine," he said softly, "if they did war that way too. No guns or things like that. Just wave your arms about a bit, sign a treaty, off you go."

That night the old man had his dream, bombs exploding, mud and blood and thunder all around. He was calling to his mates: "It's not real! Don't worry!" Waved his arms, but no-one heard him. "It's just make-believe!" he shouted til his voice was gone. But it ended just the same. It always ended just the same.

All Activity is Silent

She forgets. He forgets. She screams like a baby. He screams like a fish. They forget the screams. They forget the baby.

"Fish," she says.

"I've been," he says, and inside him a billion microbes are at work.

*

A year, another year, another year. She does not scream anymore. He thinks less of fish, notices less of her. He is surprised to see her there. Her open mouth, the tongue, the darkened teeth, the heavy breath.

"Remember?" she says, but not to him, out to the sea, the swimming buildings, words painted on their skins, but words that tell her nothing. Or, something, but she doesn't see them.

"A review," he says, and his newspaper has left a mark there on his thumb.

"You," he says.

"You," she says.

And for one moment all activity is silent and they are right right there where they belong.

Comings & Goings

A Shower of Curates
Against Joy
Carly
But If I Knew A Little More
There Is No-One In The Lab Tonight But Mice
Dissolving

"drowning in the feeling of being the imaginary lover of an imaginary man"

A Shower Of Curates

Of late years, an abundant shower of curates has fallen upon the north of England, all upon the land, and when they have earthed they stand, dust themselves off, slink away. Each has his own instructions, a map of sorts, and each has wiles and ways of translocating, spreading words and wishes. None will meet again and they feel no sorrow, not as ordinary folk might, you and I, had we been on such a journey. Have we been on such a journey? For my part, I think not. I measure my worth in these years by other means. The other day, in looking over my papers, I found in my desk the following copy of a letter, sent to me a year since by an old school acquaintance in which he bemoans – how strangely, how quite oddly! - the dearth of curates, the hollowness of temples in that time, and urges me – yes, me! – to think to join their ranks! If only I might share with him this news of the flood of them here now, of their filling of our holy – holy! – spaces, these so-called curates, these so called keepers of… Never matter now, I fear my time for medication is upon. I have just returned from a visit to my landlord - the solitary neighbour that I shall be troubled with not much longer due to… well that must wait until another. That must wait.

Ah now, that is better, the draught have done its work, its holy work, yes! I am a one for that kind, I am that since – well, if you must know that you must go back with me to the autumn of 1827, stretch yourself to parse that far, that ancient year, before all that we now know, all that we grasp as essence, as import. My godmother lived in a handsome house in the clean and ancient town of Bretton and I, being summoned, and she not being one whose summons are ignored, found myself upon her path, thinking of that very school friend I have above alluded to. My godmother was spying from her window, she attempts to hinder me in so many ways, you would surmise she wished me gone for ever. Not the kindly godmother my poor parents might have dreamed of, yet I am grateful for her challenges, they did thicken this skin of mine til today, although you might wonder at the medication I have already told of. That is another matter, purely chemical, I assure you.

"Child," said she, although I was almost a man then. And we went into her parlour, and I saw in her eye that wickedness, and henceforth were we to become conspirators. And the result? Of course, you, being sharp of mind, already know, I need not spell out for you as if we were yet in nursery and you scream and I wail and the governess... I am distracted, tangents come and flow through me. I am amiss. Godmother and I, tis we two who brought about the surge in holy – holy! – men upon the land this day, she with her alchemy and I with my own, which came from what she taught to me but which I bent to my desires.

And what of these curates now? I feel them crawling to their places, I send out webs to each in turn, they are obedience personified, although not quite person, of course!

They slink to their parishes, their teeth whiter than the whitest dentures you, my friend, will see, their smiles broad, their Biblical quotations sheer perfection.

"This," said my godmother that day, "will be our legacy, my child. Our life's work, this will be done…"

"Or undone!" I cried, for as I have mentioned I was not yet a man, but almost, and still given to outbursts. Godmother frowned and once again I was subject to her customary lecture: discretion, fewer words, secrets kept, mouths sealed shut. I blushed, lesson learnt.

I have yet varied the scheme a small amount and one curate fellow goes not to the holy place but my neighbour is even now unlocking his door to that broad smile, those Biblical quotations. It will not be long and then I shall purchase, for the matter of some small coins, the better land across that wall that I have long coveted. Godmother is not with me to see our success, or no longer corporeal, as she would have it, but she assured me she would watch from her celestial spot. Watch the foundations 'cross the land become as crumbs underfoot, the pinnings of society disease and flounder.

"Then to be reborn anew!" she said and for the one and only time, Godmother shewed her teeth, as pearls between those rosy lips.

Ah, I spy my neighbour now in conversation. Now it begins, now it is under way. I sit in my own parlour, comfortable, and I know, dear friend, that they will talk of this in decades hence, though they may never know from where it seeded, we have been so careful to obscure our part in this.

Many will attempt to write on this, volumes will be filled, I have no doubt! And all true histories contain instruction; though, in some, the treasure may be hard to find, and when found, so trivial in quantity that the dry, shrivelled kernel scarcely compensates for the trouble of cracking the nut. But men being men will keep on and on. Men being men are infinitely malleable, and were it not us, Godmother and I, it would have been some other. Our curates, they are abroad now, I sense it. Godspeed, my creatures. Godspeed, ha! Good night, my friend. Where now is my draught?

Against Joy

In the light they stay silent and still, it is in the dark that they know how to move about, how to crawl and slink. Such creatures they are, their talents are the manifestations of purpose, maybe, or of adaptation, who knows, but isn't the world the same, the weather continues hot and everything points to an early harvest. Thieving is their nature, and however much they are called to come to bed, come to sleep, come to sleep sweet one, in the night they search for gold and treasures and only once found and stored safely can they, daily, rest.

She corners one of them, she sings bad love songs in his ear and he wishes to resist his nature, just to be and be with her. But they call him, and he gets out of bed, leaves her behind to forage and pilfer with his kind. In his thoughts that night, as he lays hands on goods that he does not possess, is only her hair, and only his idea to tame a bird to light where she lives and watch her while he cannot.

When he returns, his stash well hidden, the bed is empty. The bird is gone too, and all that is left for him is to feel the daywarmth rise about him and wonder against his nature, against his talent that so prevents his joy.

Carly

Carly is a lonely child, time wandering through her like insects, and it scatters, like beetles surprised, whenever she is spoken to. When you talk to her, Carly seems to have more of everything, more features than usual, diffused, extra, spare. And yet there is not enough of her. Not enough of her to make her way in the world. As she grows older, you notice that she has stilted fingers, windy hair, wine-wet lips, and you wonder what will become of her and how time will move through her after. She becomes translucent sometimes as you watch her moving, and she is not seen by those searching for love, hunting for their mate. Carly walks beside but she is a ghost in this life, you think, and she can't be spared for long. And you are right. One day, as you see her leaving, as you see her close the front door and walk towards you, she is lifted by a gust of wind, and she is spun as if fine yarn, and taken away, upwards and outwards, and you wonder if you will ever see her again. And then, the next day and the next, you look at where she walked and you think that you had never seen anything quite as awesome as she was and you breathe these words into the wind and ask to be taken too.

But If I Knew A Little More

Bird. Bird after bird. Into and under. More birds. And then string. String pulling birds. I whistle and you. I whistle and you dive and flap and surrender.

Flap and surrender before breakfast.

Before breakfast, you leave me, again. I promise, you say, and I can hear the birds on your shoulders, in your pockets, skimming through your hair. You said that last time, I whisper, but you have already gone. The bird sitting opposite me shrugs. Sometimes, the bird seems to say, it's enough to. It's just enough.

There Is No-One In the Lab Tonight But Mice

The scientists are painting. The scientists have taken up sculpture, dancing, rock-climbing, abseiling. No-one knows why the scientists are on strike. Not just some scientists, but every scientist. All labs are closed. No science is being done at all, not by researchers, post-docs, professors, lab assistants, undergraduates. It has been going on for a while now. So, instead of experiments, the scientists are doing art, playing music, meeting in coffee shops to talk poetry.

We weren't worried at first. At first we said, They'll be back. We thought it was just some. Just those who had some sort of grievance, some grumpiness, some personality issues. We didn't know then. We didn't know it was already all of them, all at once, as if a signal had been sent that we couldn't hear, from lab to lab, whispered through pipettes, plasma tubes and particle accelerators. We should have installed devices, we thought, to listen in, to prevent. But no-one dreamed, never in our wildest planning meetings, of this.

In the press, we were upbeat, planting editorials on the right and left – money saved from all those atom-smashers, we wrote, and no more controversial GM! A simpler time, we said, who needs constant novelty? Besides, we wrote, who really understood what the scientists were doing anyway? We couldn't read their journal articles, their reports. We're better off like this, we said cheerfully.

We dispatched teams to spy on them, as they did their art, climbed rocks, discussed poems. We hung out in bowling alleys, beside lakes, in theatre upstairs bars. We hoped to hear chatter of sly research, some reactions, a result or two.

But if they were doing anything, still doing anything, they were tight-lipped.

On chat shows, the scientists laughed when asked about the strike.

"Oh, you know!" they said, and giggled. "Sometimes you just have to take a break!" And then they juggled with oranges, or formed a small human pyramid while singing sea songs in French.

After 3 months and 23 days, we had a long list of everything we were worried about: viruses (old ones becoming resistant to medication and mutating, new ones appearing); treatments for cancer, heart disease, diabetes, obesity, blindness, deafness, trembling, stiffness, pain, sadness, anger, disappointment, despair; sources of energy for when ours run out; food for when what we have runs out; immortality so our lives don't run out; bigger weapons so we can defend ourselves; antibiotics; the internet and everything on it; cars that drive themselves so we don't have to; prediction of earthquakes, volcanic activity, tectonic shifts; new ways to see inside our bodies so our cells don't run amok; the preservation of animals, birds, sea life; what's in the ocean, what's in the sky, above the skies, what's in the universe, who is out there.

After 6 months, across the world the scientists held exhibitions, performances, of what they'd been doing. They did this with the artists: they read aloud together, their art hung side by side, and on chat shows and nightly news, the scientists and the artists, their arms around each other, grinned. Not a word about ultrasounds or x-rays, about electrolysis, PCR, synaptic plasticity, antimatter, lava flow. Not a word.

We bought their art, as much as we could, and set it all out in a warehouse, then in several warehouses. Look for patterns, we instructed our teams, perhaps they're sending messages. We scoured and stripped and peered and tried to think laterally, non-laterally, out of boxes, inside boxes. We tried to see in new ways, to see deeper, wider, further. We gathered liquids, oils, sprays, scrapers, tweezers, hammers, and invented new instruments that had never been seen before, for probing, unearthing. But still we couldn't find it.

They must be trying to tell us something, we said, as we sat on the packing crates behind Warehouse 17. We had brought sandwiches, some of us had soft drinks, some had flasks of tea. We were mostly taking anti-anxiety medications by now, though we didn't tell each other. It had been 8 months and 7 days, and our panic was increasing as the pile of scientists' artworks grew. We had trouble sleeping at night, though we didn't tell each other. Some of us dreamed of viruses, some of tsunamis, some of the time before antibiotics, bodies lining the streets, aeroplanes grounded. We stopped before taking the next bite of our sandwich. We tried to smile. Smiling was difficult now.

Viruses (old ones becoming resistant to medication and mutating, new ones appearing); treatments for cancer, heart disease, diabetes, obesity, blindness, deafness, trembling, stiffness, pain, sadness, anger, disappointment, despair; sources of energy for when ours run out; food for when what we have runs out; immortality so our lives... what's in the universe, who is out there...

We were still writing editorials, still trying to sound upbeat, but were having a harder and harder time getting those done, getting the tone just right. It was a group effort now, to check we didn't inadvertently give away our fear and our misery. We had told each other about the anti-anxiety medications and also about our anxieties about the anxiety medications, of course. About them running out, about never having better ones. About. About...

We recruited volunteers to help us sort and store, with so much coming in. It was difficult, of course, to know who they were, there were so many people rushing between warehouses, of all ages, all kinds and types. We didn't pay them much attention. We had enough to worry about.

It was day 365 of the strike when she appeared. She might have been there for a while, we could have checked her armband, her electronic volunteer card. Maybe weeks or even months. But we hadn't seen her. It was 10am, we had just gathered everyone for a morning briefing, when she moved out from the crowd towards the front.

– May I? she said.

She had a piece of paper in her hand. We couldn't see what was on it. We didn't know what to say, what to do. She looked just like the other volunteers, jeans, some sort of shirt, jumper, average hair, nothing unusual. We didn't think she seemed violent. We looked at each other, then nodded.

She stood where everyone could see her. She cleared her throat, but didn't appear to be nervous. Then she said:

– I'm a post-doc. A scientist. A molecular biologist. This is from all of us. A poem. It's called "This Too Is Prayer".

And she began to read:

No, not some lover's
glance, a newborn's grin,
sunset, autumn leaves – but

this: green fluorescent
protein, a molecule
borrowed from the jellyfish
to turn our cells to
glowing dancing
labourers we applaud

as they go about
their daily tasks:
building inspection,

maintenance. Now they
have us to witness
their every act; not just,

of course, benign
construction. Not
just, of course, repair.

But how much better,
though, to see. Better
to no longer be in darkness.

Silence. There was silence. We felt something twisting in our
heads, behind our eyes. A poem. Prayer. All of them. The
scientists. This poem. Green fluorescent... Jellyfish? Jellyfish? Molecules and darkness. We were spinning. Was she
real? Was she even there? Yes, there she was, still standing.
Holding her poem. Not running, trying to escape in any
way. Comfortable. Relaxed.

– Better, she said again, to see. To no longer be in darkness.

Viruses (old ones becoming resistant to medication and mutating, new
ones appearing); new treatments for cancer, heart disease, diabetes, obe-
sity, blindness, deafness, trembling, stiffness, pain, sadness, anger...

And then, all our phones beeped at once. We looked down,
fumbled in pockets, and when we looked up again, she, the
scientist, the molecular biologist with the poem, was gone.
And on our screens we all had the same message: They're
back. In the labs and out in the field. They're back.

The scientists were back but it was different now. We watched and listened and often they brought artists with them, when they worked. Not all scientists, some of them just got straight on with what they had been doing. But in almost every country there was a poet or a painter or a video artist hanging out with the researchers, and they seemed not to be documenting, but taking part. They had lab coats, they had equipment, they joined in, although from what we could tell from our surveillance, their scientific method was not quite the same. Not less rigorous, not less dependent on repeatability, on theory and experiment. Just different.

We planted new editorials, celebrating the return of science. We were careful, of course, not to contradict any earlier pieces we had written. We knew this, how to wrangle words into the shape we needed. This we knew how to do.

The warehouses are still there, though they are locked now. We stopped examining what they contain. We shut it all up. We didn't need it any more, we thought.

We are not sure, though. We are not reassured. Many of us are still on the anti-anxiety medications, at lower doses, yes, but still. It's been months, but we can't relax. The scientists still go on chat shows, the more popular ones do the circuit, talking about their research, with artists who are collaborating. Sometimes there is juggling. Sometimes there is singing.

We don't like this situation. We want everything as it was before. We are not sure how to proceed, how to infiltrate and change it back. We have brought some of them in for questioning, and we know our international counterparts do the same, but we get nothing from them. They gladly talk about their experiments, what they are examining, the questions they are interested in now. But they won't tell us anything about why the strike happened, if it could happen again. And the artists. Why the artists?

We would like to be calm. We would like to be happy. We would like assurances, guarantees, that everything is being done as it should. Together, we try to be hopeful, but then each of us goes home alone and sits, staring at the television, out of the window. And we still have dreams, those same dreams. We are not safe in our beds any more. We take our pills and close our eyes.

*viruses (old ones becoming resistant to medication and
mutating, new ones appearing);
treatments for cancer,
heart disease,
diabetes, obesity, blindness, deafness,
trembling, stiffness, pain, sadness,
anger, disappointment, despair;
sources of energy for when ours run out;
food for when what we have runs out;
immortality so our lives don't run out;
bigger weapons so we can defend ourselves;
antibiotics;
the internet and everything on it;
cars that drive themselves so we don't have to;*

prediction of earthquakes, volcanic activity, tectonic shifts;
new ways to see inside our bodies so our cells
don't run amok;
the preservation of animals, birds, sea life;
what's in the ocean,
what's in the sky,
above the skies,
what's in the universe,
who is out there.

Dissolving

When she had had an afternoon drowning in the feeling of being the imaginary lover of an imaginary man, she took herself out to the nearest place that would fill her with liquid and she drank forever. When the last had gone, swindled away in a nonsense moment, she swayed back into the virtual streets and bound her cells for home. There, thinking he might find it comforting to hear the music he was used to, she weighted his voicemail with old 50s songs, crooning into the receiver. When hours passed and he did not answer, she curled herself up with her own double helix and dissolved back into the air.

Familiarities

Straight Up
Something Like A Tree
Flavours
We Are All Made of Protein But Some of Us Glow
More Than Others
Octopus's Garden

"they sit together on the river bed while above them the whole world teems and thrashes"

Straight Up

My father was not a slouching man. Every night when he finished dinner, he pushed back his chair and sat up straight as a rod, the way he did when demonstrating posture to his class of teenage girls at our school. He drummed his fingers on the table, tap, tap, tap, and looked at me, my shoulders, my slumped neck, the way I was shoveling mashed potato into my mouth, and I felt the heat of his discontent. He jerked his head upwards, and this was the signal. I was to instantly drop my fork and, as if some invisible cord was sliding through my spine and out the top of my head, I was to ascend. My shoulders lifted, my neck unkinked, and I grew, and as I grew, so his face softened, his brow lost its furrows and the corners of his lips lifted. He would nod his head back and forth, saying nothing. This was how it was every night. This was how it was on a good day.

I saw my father teach his class only once. I was supposed to be ill, supposed to be feverish and damply sweating into the overwashed sheets. But I was a faker and good at it. An accomplished liar by the age of ten, I knew the tricks, thermometer against light bulb, moans and groans. My mother, who couldn't miss a day at the factory, set me up with juice, water, a pile of comics and instructions to call if I vomited but otherwise to stay exactly where she left me.

Of course, I didn't. I got dressed after I heard the front

door slam, sidled downstairs and stood, breathing in the empty house, the sweet smell of freedom. What drew me to the school? It should have been the furthest thing from my mind. But I was pulled in that direction the moment I left the house.

Like a spy, I slid along walls and around corners. When I got there, I crouched beside the window of the room I knew he was teaching in. Slowly, slowly, I straightened up until the window sill was at eye level and I peeked in.

At first he didn't look like my father. The context was so strange, it was as if he was in front of one of those painted movie backdrops. He was pacing backwards and forwards by the blackboard upon which he had drawn a spine, with all its vertebrae, moving up into the neck and head. The girls were clearly not very excited about whatever he was telling them. I saw two of them passing notes, a few were chewing gum, none of them was sitting up straight. He didn't have them, they weren't eating out of the palm of his hand, not at all. They put up with him, as if he was a lost dog sniffing around their feet, but then, when the bell rang, they jumped up, grabbed their bags, streamed out of the door. And I saw my father standing by the blackboard, by his perfect drawing of a spine, standing up as straight as he could, and I could see in his face that he was hoping, straining, for some kind of reaction from them. But the girls didn't even see him. I was the only one. I was the only one who saw him standing there.

Something Like A Tree

She pushes the electronic card they gave her into the mouth of the machine. A whirr, another whirr. She looks around, and as far as she can see, stretching away across the long long hall, machines whirring and issuing commands at other small women, small men, who don't speak their language, whose English is filled with polite yesses and little else.

"Nine," commands the voice. She stares at the machine.

"Nine?"

An arm shoots out of the side of the machine, unfurls into an arrow, and where it points she sees doors, numbers. The electronic card has been ejected. She takes it, pockets it and walks slowly towards the nine.

Another machine, a table, a chair.

"Sit," and where the first voice was her schoolteacher, this voice is more like her grandfather's. She sits. She smiles. She looks around. Did anyone see her smile? Can this machine see her?

"Why have you come here?" says the grandfather-machine.

"Yes," she says, and swallows. A tissue, wiping her forehead. She is from a place of great heat, but this is not the same. The room is chilled, but she sweats.

"Why have you come here?" Grandfather-machine is measured, patient. It has all day.

"Yes," she says. She recognises the "why", the "come". She tries: "I come, to work. I come, I help."

"Your visa is for a family. What will you do for this family?"

"I clean," she says. "Yes. Old person. Grand. Mother. Help."

The grandfather-machine makes a new sound, a series of buzzing clicks. Then: a piece of paper.

"One year," says grandfather-machine. "Goodbye."

She takes the paper, which is covered in words. She stares. One year? 12 months? But she needs more, much more than that. A daughter going to university, a son in school. Years, it will take.

"But…," she says. There is no sound. Grandfather-machine is asleep. Is no longer interested. The door swings open. She understands.

The family is kind. Little children who speak too fast, much too fast, leaving her nodding, yessing, smiling, yessing, nodding. Cleaning is something she understands and she can do well, without instruction. They have a machine for this, too, but it stands in a corner and she has pressed some buttons but it seems to have broken. Every day she wants to ask why, every day she begins, in the morning, as the family have breakfast, but every day what comes out of her mouth is wrong.

The children chatter to each other, the mother and father mumble, and the grandmother doesn't speak at all. The grandmother needs cleaning, needs to be lifted, washed, dressed, and all the while the grandmother stares at something across the room. The grandmother's eyes do not move.

"It's very beautiful," she tells her daughter when they speak through the machine that is fixed to the wall in her cool room in the basement. She can see her daughter's hair, her daughter's eyes, and she has to make herself not cry. "It's like a palace, it has so many rooms!" She forces her voice into excitement, forces it to rise at the end as if this was the adventure she always dreamed of, away from her children, her familiars.

A year later, and the mother takes her to an office in the centre of the city. The mother's auto is voice-controlled, something she has never seen, something that hasn't come to her land yet. Her command of the language is improving, but here is a vehicle that speaks better than she does. She looks out of the window. She still has not discovered why the cleaning machine sits in a corner, silent; why she is needed. She still cannot ask.

In the office in the centre of the city, she nods, she says yes, yes, she smiles and smiles. Across the long long hall, she sees many machines ask questions of many small women and men. "For work," she says. "Yes, yes," she says.

A new piece of paper.

"We are so lucky!" says the mother, and she sees she has one more year.

"Yes!" she smiles, nods. Only one more year? Her daughter has two more years of university, her son five more years of school, and then.

The grandmother has not changed. She has not begun dribbling, ranting or waving her arms around. The grandmother hasn't even varied the spot on the wall at which she stares when she is lifted, washed and dressed. It is almost as if the grand-mother is not getting any older, just staying very old. The children, shoving each other, run past the open door. She has never seen them come in. She has never seen the mother or the father tell the children, "Go say hello to your grandmother". But she has seen the father come sometimes and sit in the chair in the corner. It is his mother, she thinks. He sits, with his hands on his knees, his earcam still in place in case someone should need him. Often, he says things, but so quietly that she, watching from the hallway, can't hear. He stays sometimes for an hour, and then he gets up and leaves, closing the door.

No-one touches the grandmother. Only she touches the grandmother.

She is renewed again, and then again. She speaks to her son and daughter through the machine fixed to the wall. Her son is so tall now. His voice is deep, she almost doesn't understand him and she tries so hard, tries so hard not to cry when she sees him. They used to cry when they saw her, they used to ask why she couldn't just come back, why they couldn't find another way, why did she, why was she, didn't she...? Now they just chatter and laugh and talk about friends she has never met, new places built since she left where they go to do things, things that she doesn't know but doesn't want to ask. "They will understand," her mother had said to her when she told her what she had to do, where she had to go. "They will understand."

She does not go out very much. She lifts and washes and

cleans the grandmother, cleaning the sores from the sitting, the leakings from the old, old body. She washes and cleans the grandmother carefully, thoroughly, and then she washes and cleans the house. She picks up an object, wipes underneath, and then sometimes she stands for a few moments with it in her hand, looking. Sometimes: a remote control. Sometimes: a discarded earcam. Sometimes: an animatoy. Then she puts it down and goes back to work.

While she works, she hums, melodies without words. She hums to the grandmother too, as she carefully and thoroughly washes and cleans, to make sure the grandmother knows someone is there, to keep the grandmother, to keep her from changing. She does not want anything to change. Not until her years are enough.

But soon, too soon, the grandmother is dying. It seems as though she will not be very, very old for much longer. When the grandmother tries to breathe there is a dark deep knocking from inside as if something wants to leave. Doctors come, scanning with their tools, but still, there is no stopping death. The mother is looking at the father. The father is looking at the doctor. The children are not home much anymore. Finally, the father nods, the doctor nods, and they go into the grandmother's room.

She is not needed. She stands in the hall outside, and then she stands back when they come to take away the grandmother, the grandmother's eyes closed now, no more knocking inside her chest. She reaches out a hand towards the grandmother. "Yes," she says. "Yes."

The mother is very sorry. The mother says something fast, and then she says it slower, about "carer allowance", about "not being able to", about "so sorry". Then there is a new machine in the middle of the room, a new cleaning machine, and they are saying, "Take a few days," and she is packing up, telling her children through the machine fixed to the wall in her cool room in the basement that she will let them know when, let them know where.

The mother's auto drops her off in the centre of the city. She stands outside the doors to the building which gave her a piece of paper every year, just one more year. She reaches out her hand and the doors slide open towards the long long hall with the machines and the small women and small men, but her legs take her backwards and she turns and walks away. Walks away with her small bag of nothing in it and her small purse with the electronic card, enough for a few meals, a few days.

She walks down the bright street, and she turns a corner and another corner. She walks until there are no more walls and no more screens and no more autos and no more sliding doors or machines with pieces of paper.

She hopes for something like a tree. She hopes for some animals. She hopes for someone to talk to. In her head she speaks to herself in her own language, but after so long, after so many years, it is mixed up. It is filled with yesses and bits that have stuck to her from conversations: "detergent", "allowance," "earcam", "my turn," "bedsores", "homework". Her head is full of these sticky words, and what use is she now?

She stops walking. The road is everywhere, stretching on both sides. There is no grass. There are no animals. She has her small bag of nothing in it and her small purse with the electronic card and her head full of things that aren't hers, and she has no future and her past is dissolving. She sits down, just sits, right there on the road, and waits for someone to come and tell her what to do next.

Flavours

The boy and his father met, every Saturday, for ice cream. It was always Saturday and it was always ice-cream. In winter, they sat inside and fought to finish before central heating caused a meltdown; in summer they had a favourite bench.

The first time, the boy did not know what these were, these tubs, these coloured slabs. He looked up at his father, who had already ordered, and then guessed, pointing. The cold sweetness stunned the boy's mouth and teeth. His father grinned so the boy grinned back.

Over the years, the flavours they chose varied. The boy began with the classics: chocolate, vanilla, strawberry, and his father teased him as he licked his pistachio, his mint choc chip. The boy would ask for a taste, would scrunch up his face in mock disgust, and laugh along with his father's too-loud guffaws, out of the corner of his eye watching the others, with their cones, making everything look so easy.

When the boy was a teenager, he wanted to meet on a different day, his Saturdays became precious, but knew he couldn't ask. So he sat, with one scoop of coffee and one of raspberry, waiting for his father to hold forth on bizarre flavour combinations. His father's laugh was still as loud; the boy's embarrassment growing as he did.

When the boy went away to college, at first his father would telephone on Saturdays and they would still eat ice cream together at a distance, each describing it to the other. But after a few months, the boy would just pretend, looking out of the window while his father talked, murmuring a response. Then, a while after that, the boy stopped staying in on Saturdays and the phone, he supposed, just rang and rang.

When the boy was no longer a boy, he became a father himself. His wife knew not to suggest ice cream, not to buy it, and their house became one of cakes, of biscuits, of warm puddings and hot sauces. His wife also knew not to ask too much of the boy, or of his father when the father was still around.

As his own daughter grew, the boy found himself thinking more of those Saturdays and developing, years after he had stopped, a taste again, for the classics: chocolate, strawberry, vanilla. Taking his daughter out to give his wife an hour alone in a quiet house, the boy, who was no longer a boy, found himself where the ice cream shop had been. Instead, there were shoes. The boy stood and stared at the display of sandals, boots and high heels.

His daughter pulled him away to chase after a small dog. As they followed the dog and the dog's owner across to the park, the boy, not a boy anymore, a father now himself, tasted pistachio, mint choc chip. Then his daughter screamed with laughter, tugged her father's hand, and his mouth, suddenly, was dry. "Come on," he said to her, whirling her up into his arms. "Come on."

We Are All Made Of Protein But Some Of Us Glow More Than Others

At first when she looks down the eyepiece she sees nothing, only blackness. "Mum," he says, and moves her hand to show her how to focus. Sarah turns the knob and suddenly there's a pulsing: the fish's heart! Her own beats up in time. So small, so magnified. She sees lots of tiny dots, all glowing green. One dot moves, it makes a dash along. "Immune cells," he whispers by her ear. She's watching like it's television. The creature's inner workings. "Beautiful," she says, her boy, her son, standing proud as if he built this microscope, made this tiny zebrafish. "How?" she says, as the green dots shift and shuffle. "How?"

The jellyfish's name is Aequorea Victoria. When the young scientist hears this, he thinks of the old English queen. He wonders if the current queen, the one who was crowned only a few years before, would like her own jellyfish. He is in Princeton, listening to his new supervisor, hearing words like "squeezate". Squeezate, he thinks, from, squeeze, squeezed, squeezing. A squeeze expanded, lengthened out; an old word moulded into novelty. The young scientist hasn't yet met one of these jellyfish, or even thousands. He hasn't yet made the seven-day journey with his wife in the back of his supervisor's new car across so many states, or lain in the rowboat on the harbour, looking at the clouds.

The young scientist tries to listen again to the older man, not to think about all that might be, all that he doesn't know, the questions he might ask.

Sarah giggles and shrieks because her friends do. Giggling, shrieking, as they lift each one from the bucket. That first summer, hauling each creature out with both hands, whispering, twitching. Her friends shriek and giggle as they do this but Sarah doesn't find them odd or cool or creepy. She likes the heavy weight, as if it is a pudding or a pillow, but living, or once lived. As she lifts it gently out and holds it there, she imagines something passing between it and her, and while it does she doesn't make a sound. She stands quite still and lets it pass.

The young scientist is watching them as he lifts from his own bucket. He hopes the girls obey his guidelines; he is paying them, he is expecting that, he is hoping that they take some care. This is no outing to the shopping mall, he hopes they understand. His own small children do it well, and they are younger, but they are slow and careful, cutting only what should be cut and not missing anything that must be there. The scientist has wished that he could do this alone, at one side of the quiet laboratory. But he needs such quantities, so many creatures, just to get the smallest part, some drops to test; he requires an army of assistants. His mouth turns down slightly. He picks up his scissors and reaches into the bucket.

The young scientist lies back in the rowboat and dreams. He dreams himself under the water and among them. Why do they glow? And why not just use the blue light they emit, why that next step which turns it into green? Aequorea Victoria do not answer him. One dream he has: tiny fireflies upon each jellyfish, sitting on the creatures' skin, waking up when agitated. Another dream: the glow is like a match being struck, an underwater match. Perhaps the glowing ones are like beacons guiding in errant flyers like an airport runway. Perhaps they are marking places of great importance. He does not dismiss these as nonsense, he doesn't laugh at anything. This is his thinking, this is how it works. He looks up at the clouds and continues to dream.

She has seen him, the young scientist, in the rowing boat. Sarah has stood on the jetty on her way back from school and seen him lying there, just floating, bobbing, floating. At first she thought the boat was empty, out there on its own. She moved to where she had a better view and then she saw him, eyes maybe open, or maybe not. She stood for a long time: what is he doing, what is he thinking about? But he was thinking nothing, emptying out his mind as far as possible. What he wasn't thinking about: his wife, jellyfish, the tension in the lab, the blue light, the green glow, how.

Another man, in another time, thinks only: worms. Worms are his field, c. elegans, a lovely name for something unlovely. A transparent worm. He is thinking of them as he walks towards the hall in which the seminar will be held, wondering about them as he sits in his place, at the end of a row in the middle. He is not expecting much from today. This is what he is not expecting: glowing, insight, protein, green, revolution. When he hears what he hears, he stops listening and begins to imagine.

There is a boy who wants to take Sarah to the movies. This is the first boy who has asked her. This is the first time. Her friends giggle at this and nudge and tickle her and she likes that they giggle because she can too and inside her is a big shriek waiting to come out. A boy and the movies and a boy in there with her, sitting by her! It will be this Saturday, her mother and father have allowed it, after some discussion, after some questions regarding the boy. The discussions did not happen in front of her, they were in the kitchen while she sat still on the sofa, not thinking. What she was not thinking about: Simon, his hands, his funny smile, his arm next to hers, her stomach, the big shriek inside.

In the rowing boat, he is trying again not to think. Of Aequorea Victoria, of blue and green and glowing. So instead he thinks of his daughter, how she is enjoying school, how she is speaking like an American already, using words he doesn't know, and this makes him happy. His son is not so forward, and the young scientist smiles at this too, because it was like that for him. He closes his eyes and there in his mouth is that taste, his wife made it for their dinner, after the fried chicken. A recipe from the friendly neighbour who thinks perhaps they eat the jellyfish, who is worried for them. This makes the young scientist almost laugh, he knows it is what many of them think. Eating the jellyfish! But what they had last night was like meringue but not so hard, and then – the sweetness! The lemon sweetness, and he can taste it again, filling his mouth. Wait. And he sits up, the boat rocking.

Simon has chosen the movie and Sarah is happy about this because she doesn't want to have to do anything. He has kept his hands in his pockets and then, when he stands by the end of their row and lets her walk down first, his arm hovers slightly as if he was going to touch. Sarah slides along, her legs rubbing the seat backs as she moves to the middle of the movie theater, then two more along so there is no-one in front. She sits and Simon is still standing, and she looks up towards him and his mouth is turned in an odd way that makes her think he is happy and her skin is tingling and in her stomach is a glow.

There is tension in the lab air. The young scientist doesn't know the expression about cutting it with a knife, but if he did he would repeat it to himself because this is how it feels. He has a new theory but it is not agreed with. This has not been the expectation, that the younger disagrees with the older, that there is disharmony. This has not been said in words, but it has been implied strongly and the young scientist is disappointed. This is not how science is, following along, agreeing. Of course, he cannot say this, he is here on someone else's invitation, an invitation that comes with money, that comes with certain assumptions. But he is not being blocked. Just disapproved of, and that is something he can live with. So the supervisor carries on grinding tissues, with his assistant, sticking to the path already known, while across the room, the young scientist walks another road, in darkness, looking for some small light to justify rebellion.

Sarah is on her own today. Her friends decided not to come, they tried to make her join them, they teased and prodded but she didn't want to go where they were going. So it is just her and her bucket, no giggles or shrieks, just quiet persever- ance. Take one out, carefully carefully cut around its edge, its fringe. She has instructions, what to do, was not told the why of it, but doesn't mind. The small amount they pay her makes her feel grown-up, she's saving it for something special. While she holds the jellyfish and cuts around, she thinks of pearls, her mother's, that she is not allowed to touch but only sometimes, when her mother has a party. When she was small, she tried to grab and got a slap on her hand, which hurt. When she's older, will she be allowed? Sarah looks down at where she's cutting. "I'm sorry," she whispers, as the scissors slice.

It works! The young scientist has done it, and now he shows his boss, the man who brought him here, who drove them across so many states, that long long drive of seven days. The young scientist has found what they were trying to isolate, thanks to lemons, to thoughts that began with lemons, citric acid, PH difference. It is not what anyone imagined. Back in his home country, he had researched lights and glows in other creatures but this one is different. Differently luminous, and now he has found it, isolated what makes it shine. He needs more samples to study it, this new protein, which he will soon call "aequorin". He needs buckets of jellyfish, armies of assistants at the docks, scooping them up. The young scientist makes sure not to grin at all when he shows his results to the older man, but inside he is smiling so much that there is an ache. Lemons.

Sarah is pregnant, a great roundness already so that she is slightly off balance. Her husband, who is not Simon, who came a while after that first one, the scratchy movie seats, the first lookings up and down, is away a great deal and Sarah is mostly on her own. She stands in front of the bedroom mirror and cups her hands underneath her stomach, feeling something pass between her and herself. "Come on," she says, waiting for emergence.

The man who thinks only of worms has tried it once, it took several weeks and many steps, but something didn't work and under the microscope: darkness. He shone the blue light, strained his eyes for something, but only black. So he began again, with new worms, breeding them up with the protein, tagging the cells. And then, weeks later again, more weeks, he slides the tiny creature under, focusses, shines the blue light, and it's there. Green glowing cells, dashing about. For the first time, he sees inside. He sits there quietly, watching his living worm.

Sarah is behind her easel in her studio, which is really just an extension of the kitchen. Her paintings are bought and sold often enough, someone has called them "silently luminous", although to her they are very loud. She is creating this one for her son, to go in his new apartment. She stares for a while, then puts the brush down, pushes back her chair with some effort and goes into the kitchen. It is early, the morning show is playing, with muted sound, on the television on the counter, and as she switches on the kettle, she sees it: jellyfish. She stands quite still, and feels it again in her hands, sees them in the buckets, hears her friends giggling. An old face on the screen, but something speaks to her, of rowing boats and scissors, of hours in laboratories cutting. They're saying that he's won, and she's not convinced the face is him, but she thinks that it just might be. She switches up the volume, forgets about the tea, the kettle. They talk about his prize, what he has done, and as they do they show the pictures, little green glowing cells, and Sarah watches, listens and remembers.

The jellyfish's name is Aequorea Victoria. When the young scientist hears this, he thinks of the old English queen. He wonders if the current queen, the one who was crowned only a few years before, would like her own jellyfish. He hasn't yet met one of these jellyfish, or even thousands. He hasn't yet made the seven-day journey with his wife in the back of his supervisor's new car across so many states, or lain in the rowboat on the harbour, looking at the clouds. The young scientist tries to listen again to the older man, not to think about all that might be, all that he doesn't know, the questions he might ask.

Octopus's Garden

As she slips into her wetsuit and adjusts her tank, she decides on this week's alphabet game. *Across the Universe*, she thinks as she dives. *All You Need is Love. A Hard Day's Night.* Wait, what if it's *Hard Day's Night*? Or even *It's Been a Hard Day's Night*? Her mind a blank, she heads for the riverbed.

After some careful scrabbling, she finds what she's been sent for – a wedding ring – comes back up, and hands it in. She's not permitted to return it to the client, but hears that he said it "just slipped off my finger as I was leaning over." Don't believe him, lady, she thinks as she walks home. She likes to walk after a plunge. Trains and buses are terra not so firma.

All Together Now comes as she turns her key in the lock; *Blackbird* while she heats the soup, and, just before dropping off to sleep, *Can't Buy Me Love*.

The squad practice airless rescues in a floor-to-ceiling pool. When she mentions this during dinner with a man she has just met, he starts to hyperventilate. She stands and motions to a waiter, who gets a paper bag for him to breathe into. She listens while he gulps for air and thinks how odd it is, as they are both on land. When he is breathing normally again, he crumples up the paper bag and asks quickly for the bill. He doesn't look her in the eye. She doesn't know if this is from shame or disgust.

She loves the floor-to-ceiling pool. It's in the bottom of

an ancient building – not designed for swimming, of course. Something to do with supporting the foundations. They work in pairs, taking turns to need salvation. She shares her breathing apparatus, moving it from her mouth to her colleague's then back again. It never strikes her that she could die. It never has.

At parties, she finds it hard to talk about what she does.

"I dive," she will say and waits as they bring up beaches, sun, and surf. "For the council," she will add.

"Oh," they'll say. "I haven't heard of that." Then comes: "Buried treasure, eh?" They sweep her body with their dry eyes and say, "Bet you look nice in a wetsuit."

She will mumble, slip away, spike her orange juice with gin or vodka, and sigh, on a balcony if she can find one. Later, the friend that made her come that night will say, "Where did you get to? I wanted you to meet…" She will shake her head and in their shared taxi she will gaze out of the window at the river as they drive home.

Sometimes, when she wakes up in the middle of the night and can't get back to sleep, she stands, naked, by her window, holding her wetsuit like a second skin.

During training they took a psych course.

"What makes people jump from bridges?" said the instructor, a cool woman in a short skirt, sitting on the desk, legs crossed.

"Unrequited love," said a man at the back, and the instructor said, "Yes! Exactly, number one! What else?"

She wondered what the hell this was for. It's not like she was going to counsel them as she dragged them to the surface. She drew dolphins in the margins of her notebook.

"Financial ruin," said the instructor. "Clinical depression. A row with a loved one. A belief in immortality."

At this, she lifted her head, looked towards the front. Immortality. No one else seemed bothered. She raised her hand.

"Yes?" said the instructor, recrossing her legs.

"A bad night's sleep," she whispered. "A disappointing meal. A lack of connection."

"Sorry," said the instructor. "Could you speak up?"

She wrote a story once for a school assignment, about a boy who lived with mermaids. It didn't end well. The mermaids left him alone one day, telling him to stay in the cave. But he swam up to the surface, breathed the air and died, sinking slowly down and down until he landed, blue, on the bottom.

Her teacher wrote, "Beautiful images! Why so sad?"

The next dive is for someone's necklace. *Day Tripper*, she thinks as she plummets. *Dear Prudence*, and her hand reaches for something glittering but it's not what she's been sent for. Someone else's jewels. Someone who doesn't want them back, doesn't bother.

She hides in the next room, listening to the owner of the necklace and the husband, who is screaming at his wife. I need sex, she thinks while peeling off her wetsuit. *Drive My Car*, she hums on her way home.

The next time it's another wedding ring. On the way down: *Eight Days a Week, Eleanor Rigby*, and *For No One*. On the way up – *Get Back* – she decides to follow the careless husband. Just to see. But when she listens from the next room, it's a woman.

She follows anyway, walking a few steps behind. The woman has long blonde hair and smells of peaches. She follows the woman into a nearby café. She sits a few tables away and watches. They both order coffee. When she finishes, she thinks, This is ridiculous, and leaves. She starts to walk home. But a few minutes later she smells peaches, then there is warm breath in her ear. Someone takes her hand.

They go to her flat. They have never done this before, they say; her and someone else's wife. The woman is bolder than she is and they find they fit together, there is no fumbling, no clashing limbs.

As she groans and aches, a part of her is standing by the chair, holding the wetsuit, watching.

They sit, dressed, in the kitchen. The woman is talking about her husband.

"If you met him, you would understand," the woman says. The woman tells her where the husband works, what time he leaves each day, what he will be wearing, which way he will head. She is to stand outside. She is to collide with him. Just to know.

She does what she is told. She waits and he comes out and she bumps into him. He is like marble, cold. And thin, like paper.

"So sorry," she says, looking straight at him. He doesn't

smile. He doesn't apologize. He nods. He walks around her and carries on towards the station. But his eyes In his eyes: Something she knows. *Hello Goodbye.*

She tells the wife that she met him. She tells the wife what the wife wants to hear. They share a bed again, and again they fit. She doesn't mention what else she saw.

They meet up several times over the next few weeks. They go to bed and then they sit, dressed, in the kitchen, while the wife talks about her husband. She makes sure to appear to be listening, but she is somewhere else: Beatles songs, floor-to-ceiling pools, wetsuits, and boys brought up by mermaids.

She goes away, on a holiday of sorts, to see her parents. During the day she sunbathes, lying on a towel spread out on the floor of their empty swimming pool. The sun burns her, bouncing off the desiccated pool tiles.

"It's the drains," her mother says at dinner when she asks what happened to the water. Her father grunts his disagreement, and they start to argue.

She finishes her salad, picks up her wine glass and goes outside to look at stars and think of someone else's husband.

Three days after she is back at work it happens. An emergency call. Two passenger ferries. She slides her wetsuit on and, with the rest of the squad, she dives. She doesn't play a game as she goes down. She doesn't think of anything.

The water is churning with panic. She dives deeper, underneath the second ferry, and that is where she finds him. He is in his suit. He is holding tight to his briefcase. He is not marble anymore, not paper.

She takes out her mouthpiece, gives it to him, and as he breathes they look at each other. They share oxygen but they do not rise. She does not pull him to the surface; he does not ask to go. She breathes, then he breathes, then she, until there is no more left. Then she lets the mouthpiece drop away and he releases his briefcase, takes off his suit, his tie.

She reaches out her hand, he takes it, and they sit together on the riverbed while above them the whole world teems and thrashes.

In Theory

Experimentation
Hold The Baby
The Evolutionary Imperative of Laughter is
                                    Confused
The House of Meat
If Kissed By A Dragonfish
The Most New Sport
The Party

"It listens very closely, and then slowly, ever so slowly, it begins to grow."

Experimentation

12.03pm

He sits at the microscope, counting bacteria. He hears her coming. She stands by his bench. She picks up a pipette.

"I'd rather you didn't do that," he says.

"Oh," she says. "OK." And she puts the pipette back and walks off.

He writes in his notebook: *12.03 I say: "I'd rather you didn't do that." She says "oh", "ok".* He sets his timer for half an hour.

12.33pm.

He sits at the microscope, counting bacteria. He hears her coming. She stands by his bench. She picks up a pipette. He looks up. He smiles at her.

"Hi," he says.

"Oh," she says. "Sorry, I was just…" and she puts the pipette back and walks off.

He writes in his notebook: *12.33 I say "hi". She says "oh, sorry I was just".* He sets his timer for half an hour.

1.03pm

He sits at the microscope, counting bacteria. He hears her coming. She stands by his bench. She picks up a pipette. He looks up. He holds out his hand. She slowly places the pipette in his palm as if it were a small animal. She grins. He nods. She walks off.

He writes in his notebook: *1.03 I hold out my hand. She says nothing. Hands over the pipette. Grins.*

That's enough for today. He puts the plates of bacteria away and goes into the office, where he sits down at his laptop and records the new results. He decides that for the rest of the week he will make more variations. Tomorrow, he will wear a lab coat. Thursday he will vary the time intervals by leaving the room shortly after each encounter. On Friday, he will turn the lab radio to another station.

He gets up to go for lunch. She is sitting at the other end of the office, her back to him, listening to something on her headphones. As he leaves the room he remembers how it felt as she handed him back the pipette, her warm fingers touching his cold palm.

Hold the Baby

They said she had to hold the baby so she held the baby even though she had no notion why she held it, him or her. They said she couldn't look to see so in her mind she thought of it as both, a Jenny and a James, and she knew it wasn't right but there was nothing more to say. They said they'd run some tests while she was holding it, experiments of a sort, but she was not so clear on what sort. Perhaps they measured angles, how she held it, how it sat there. Maybe they counted breaths, hers and its, or maybe blood flow or pressure, with machines she couldn't see. Maybe they wired up her brain and knew what she was thinking, feeling. Some time had passed, maybe minutes, and then she wanted to drop the baby. Not hard, not on the floor, just to not hold it any more.

The Evolutionary Imperative of Laughter Is Confused

She laughed and her laughing made me nervous, I was trying to help her and didn't know: was she delighted or hys-
terical? I didn't want to stop trying to help her, our time was
bounded, she was a stranger to me and had come; I offered
services. She laughed, I pointed to her work, I laughed, and
then, towards the end, as we were drawing the close closer
and I had almost finished, had nothing more to say, she said,
I haven't laughed so much for ages, and I said, Oh, thank
goodness, I didn't know! I said, I didn't know if it was a
good sign, and she laughed at that too, and she stood up
and I stood up, we moved towards the door, and she was
smiling and we said goodbye. I could hear her, all the way
down the stairs.

The House of Meat

The meat in the petri dish won't do anything when watched, so Dick and Ellen switch the camera on and leave. On their way up from the lab, Ellen says:

"Dick."

"Hmm?" says Dick.

"What if the fucking meat never bloody grows?"

"Oh ye of little…," says Dick, who's known for not finishing his sentences. Ellen sometimes helps him finish, after hours, in the coffee room, when they think their boss has left.

And what of the meat? It's no more than a meaty smudge, millimetres across. Not meat so much yet as meat essence, tiny meaty cells gathered on a dish. Is this flesh? Is one meat cell alive?

Dick, Ellen, and Larry, their boss, have had this discussion.

"Fuck it," Ellen said. "Does it really matter?"

"Ha, matter!" said Dick. "The stuff of life. What a piece of work is man, how noble in…"

"I prefer to think of it as meat precursor," said Larry, who knows what Dick and Ellen do sometimes in the coffee room, after hours. He doesn't mind. He is in favour of workplace sex. Shame that he has only himself to have it with right now. An ex-wife and four kids. He sometimes wonders whether the children are ex- too. They sneer when he takes them out, singly or in groups, no matter how many burgers he allows them, no matter how thick the milkshakes. Larry is learning how a sneer from your child can suck the marrow from your bones.

"I think it makes a difference," Larry said. "How we treat it, how we perceive it while we work. Dick?"

Dick – on his second post-doc and with dreams of his own lab – is a serial agreer. He thinks maybe he should, every now and then, raise hell, just to demonstrate some backbone. But he has no idea how.

"Sure," he said. "Ellen, I mean, didn't you have that with your fish? I mean, what if you hadn't thought of them as fish at all?"

Ellen hadn't liked the zebrafish in her last lab. Slimy, see-through buggers. She would have preferred a mouse, or even fruit flies, although they get up your nose and in your sandwiches. But that was what the funding was allocated for and so she bred and bred the little bastards. They seemed to stop reproducing early, as if they sensed her disgust. She'd had the devil of a time getting hold of more with the particular gene knocked out. She's happier here, with meat. Or meat precursor.

"What the hell else would I have thought they were?" she said, and Dick wondered, once again, why he let her do what she did to him. Then he grinned, remembering two nights earlier.

"What's so funny?" Ellen said.

Larry sensed the situation deteriorating, much like the

last meat precursor. It had micro-shuddered, looked as if it might splutter into action, and then wheezed and solidified. They threw it away and began again.

Ellen stuck a Post-It with the word "Spooks" on the door.

"It's not exactly like there's a bank of monitors, like we're watching every move, for god's sake," she says when Larry sets up their "surveillance" in a former cupboard. "It's meat. In a dish. What's it going to do?"

But right now, this is the place of greatest excitement. Of hope. Of funding dreams.

"Come in, folks!" says Larry, who has deliberately not sat right by the solitary screen. To encourage them to take an interest. Just like kids, he thinks. Shit.

Ellen grabs a chair and pulls in close, slamming her hand on the camera's tilt and zoom. Dick decides not to say anything. Like he ever would.

The meat is making decisions too. Feeling unwatched, feeling more comfortable, it instructs a solitary cell to multiply. Test out the water, so to speak. They've changed the nutrient mix, they've adjusted the medium, they've tried to make things palatial for the smudge to grow into steak.

The meat is almost convinced.

Larry gets a phone call, heads back to the office. Dick and Ellen sit there for an hour. There's not much else to do.

"Dick," says Ellen.

"Hmm," says Dick.

Ellen puts her hand on his crotch.

"Oh," says Dick. Damn, he thinks. I have no willpower, I have no willpower. I have no...

Larry decides to organize a Lab Day Out. He takes them to an abattoir, to illustrate the point of their research.

"Oh my!" Ellen says, eyeing up the carcasses. She wants to do Dick, right there in their nylon hats, their nylon coats and bacteria-proof booties. But Dick is going green and Larry steers them through more quickly.

"Educational, eh?" he says, a hand on Dick's wobbling shoulder. "Imagine all this – gone! Fields here instead, a children's playground..." A quick flash of sneer appears in his mind. He shoves it away.

"Like building on a graveyard," says Ellen. Dick leans against the nearest wall, breathing hard.

Larry decides Lab Day Out Number One should draw to a close. It hasn't been the post-failure morale boost he had hoped.

The meat is confused. The meat has seen the camera. The cells that were sent to explore have transmitted back that things are comfortable, that it might be conducive. The meat decides not to take a firm stance yet, and dispatches another party.

Dick wants to ask Ellen out for dinner. He rehearses in his head while he eats his re-heated vegetarian lasagne. Dick keeps remembering the abattoir. He hopes this won't last forever because eating meat is one of his only pleasures. He doesn't like the way the vegetables swim in the cheesy sauce. It's not right.

Larry watches Dick's lips move from across the office. Larry has no real sense of whether he likes Dick or not, which is odd. He has always felt something for his postdocs. He always wants them to be part-friendly, part-antagonist. To follow instructions and also, every now and then, to do something radical, take initiative. He's not sure what happened in this mix but the balance seems off. He watches Dick talk to himself and imagines Dick running his own lab. No, he can't imagine it. Well, maybe if Dick had a very quiet grad student. Not a woman. Better not. Then he imagines Dick and Ellen with a house, a garden and three kids. No, he can't see that either. Larry turns back to his funding application. "Creating meat in the laboratory has vast implications for future populations," he types for the umpteenth time.

Dick gets up and moves towards Ellen. Ellen has a sign that says "Do No Disturb" hanging on the back of her chair, but it's always there so Dick isn't sure whether he can or not. He stops halfway, then goes to the loo instead.

Ellen hasn't noticed any of this.

Ellen's friends invite her to see a piece of performance art. A naked woman, the artist, is sitting with a large and dead pig on her lap. The artist invites gallery visitors to touch: either her, the pig, or both.

Ellen shrieks with laughter at first, then decides that the whole thing is gruesome, but when persuaded by her friends, she runs her fingers along the animal's back and puts a tentative hand on the artist's thigh. The experience unnerves Ellen so much she needs a stiff drink. Skin and skin and skin, what are we? is the thought that whisky can't quite get rid of.

Ellen thinks of this as she sits alone in the surveillance room and watches the meat. You're me and I'm you, she tells it. She looks at her arm and imagines it on a plate, medium rare. The arm doesn't work, so she stands up, unzips her jeans and pulls them down. She traces a finger around her right thigh in the shape of a steak. It takes a while, but then she sees it, just like one of those pictures which snap into focus when you relax your eyes.

Dick comes in, sees Ellen with her trousers down. His eyes widen.

"Piss off," says Ellen.

Dick leaves.

Ellen turns to the monitors.

"What are you looking at?"

The meat says nothing.

For their next Lab Day Out, after the fifth meat failure, Larry takes them to a meeting in London with another lab, potential collaborators. He hopes that the enthusiasm in the room will infect his group. On the train, Ellen picks her nails and stares out of the train window. Dick stares at Ellen. Larry feels despair.

Things do not go well. Larry is forced to do all the talking at the meeting. His postdocs seem to have taken a vow of sulkiness. The other group is clearly not impressed.

"Thanks so much," says Larry, shaking the professor's hand. He almost wants to shove Dick and Ellen, remind them of their manners.

It is no surprise when the other group doesn't follow up the meeting with any further suggestions.

It's also not much of a surprise when Ellen quits.

"I can't do this stuff any more," she tells Larry, standing by his desk, hands on hips. Larry says something about research into artificial meat being a long term endeavour, about patience.

"It's not just the meat, it's everything going wrong!" says Ellen, who looks to Larry like she might cry. "I can't stand it, how can anyone live like this? I mean, can you promise me something, anything, is ever going to work? And even if it does, that someone else won't beat us to it and it'll be for nothing? Nothing!"

Her voice is rising to a shriek. Larry is a little worried.

"I wish…," he says. "I wish I could, I really… But science is, you know, it's just, it's trial and…"

"Science," says Ellen. And this is a sneer, an almost perfect sneer. "I've had it with bloody science. I'm going to retrain."

"Oh," says Larry. "You're… really?" He's stunned. Ellen is good. Not great, but she has a certain feel for it all, an intuition. "I'm sorry to hear that, really. But of course, if you need it, I'll write you any reference you want. I'm sorry, I really am."

At this, Ellen gets a tissue from her sleeve and blows her nose.

"Thanks," she mumbles. "It's not you… I mean. Thanks. Bye."

There is no grand farewell with Dick. He stands by her desk while she shoves things into a bag.

"Are you...?" he says. "Would you maybe like to... sometime?"

Ellen looks up at him. "You're joking, right?"

But when she's finished, when her desk is just a mess of Post-It notes and empty chocolate wrappers, she picks up her bag and, on her way out, she pats him, quite hard, on the shoulder. Dick isn't sure but he thinks she mumbled something like, "You were the most fun part," but really, it could have been anything. He watches her slouch down the corridor, push through the swing doors. Dick sighs.

Dick starts eating meat again. And when he starts, he can't stop. He eats every part of every animal he can find: pigs' trotters, liver, heart, spleen, beef cheeks. He feels himself changing inside, as he ingests more and more flesh. He finds restaurants which pride themselves on dishes with intestines, brains, testicles, and he savours it all.

At one meal, he finally notices that the waitress is smiling at him. After turning to check it isn't aimed at the guy behind, he smiles back, his mouth full of sweetbreads.

With Dick now keeping strictly office hours, Larry takes to coming back in the evenings, after going home or suffering interminable, sometimes violent, yes-you-have-to-see-your-father meals with the kids.

At first, he sits in the surveillance room, but after a few days he moves into the lab, right by the apparatus.

Then he starts to talk.

"Did I tell you," he says, "about the night Eddie was born? The happiest day of my life, really. When they handed him to me..."

He keeps talking.

And the meat? What of the meat?

The meat listens. It listens very closely, and then slowly, ever so slowly, it begins to grow.

If Kissed By A Dragonfish

If kissed by a dragonfish, do not bite. If kissed by a dragonfish, make sure you are sitting. If kissed by a dragonfish,
let it sway you. Do not worry about a scale or two you may
have to pick out from between your teeth. Do not worry
during the kiss, before the kiss, or after. The dragonfish's
skin is armoured but its heart beats loud and soft. You will
not forget the kiss. You will not forget the coolness of the
dragonfish's breath inside your lungs. You will look down
through the floor of glass and see nothing, swimming. You
will part, like an ocean, and on your sea bed you will pearl.

The Most New Sport

When there is a New Sport they find the players to fit: Elongated for basketball; sleek for swimming; flexibly-jointed for golf. Put the elongated, the sleek and the flexibly-jointed in a room, at an awards ceremony, say, and the elongated will not be able to bend to hear what the sleek are saying, while the flexibly-jointed raid the buffet table from many novel angles.

But this Most New Sport is confusing. The inventors, the ones with imaginations ranging wild and heads for rules, constructs, gaming, are not in agreement over who is the Ideal Player. This Most New Sport needs stretching, but also shrinking, speed and slowness, cunning, selfishness, and a team-like spirit. Keep one eye on the ball while gripping a bat-like, racket-like, swinging it, skipping, shuffling.

"Too complicated!" wails the child of one of the inventors, rubbing bruises where the newly designed part-rubber, part-felt ball hit knees, stomach, right ear. The child sniffles off. The inventors look at each other, mouths lemoned. They are overwhelmed by pressure to do this. They do not sleep at night, dreaming of their Most New Sport.

After the child has gone, to relax they have a quick game. As they run, crawl, whack, slide, tap and saunter, all their stress grows wings.

"We love this," they say to each other, knowing, knowing, knowing that what they have invented would change everything. *Everything*.

They have money men (and one woman) who were "mightily impressed" when they watched the two inventors play. They reached for their devices and swiftly turned out a tiny part of their electronic pockets into the inventors' bank account.

"Get it out there," they instructed. "Get it into parks and onto courts, spark up our youth. We need a new way to..." At this the money men – and woman – looked at one another, and each inventor felt again like the child in the playground, the one no-one invited to join in. Each inventor thought, "This time, I *am* the game", but the child inside shuddered.

A year later, and the inventors must admit they just can't do it. No-one else can play their New Sport. No-one else can take on even a few of the rules, the must-dos and the can't-dos. They have travelled everywhere, cajoled all sorts and types and heights, widths and flexibilities, but they have failed.

It seems only they can play it.

So they play and play, each winning, losing, winning, and eventually, all thoughts of money men and woman, of bringing their New Sport to the world, to parks and courts, all ideas of fame and immense fortunes, fade and vanish. They just play on and on.

"We love this," they say to one another, as they run, crawl, whack, slide, tap and saunter, grinning, the young inventors playing the Most New Sport designed just for two.

The Party

We get to the party. We say hello to our hosts. We take off our coats. The party is crowded. We fight our way through to the kitchen. We load our plates with food. We sit in a corner. There are a lot of people. There are mathematicians and physicists, experimentalists and theoreticians. There is an elderly but still lively Nobel prize-winner. We are not mathematicians, we are not physicists. When someone asks what we do, we swallow our food and we say, *biochemists*. They are polite, they nod, but they change the subject. They talk about a film they have seen or about the décor of the kitchen. We nod, we talk politely too, even though we have not seen that film.

At a certain point, there is music, quite loud, from the other room. We place our plates on the side and move into the hallway. We see people, dancing: mathematicians, physicists, theoreticians and experimentalists, and the elderly but still lively Nobel prize-winner. We look at each other and then we sneak up the stairs. We find the room where the coats are kept and we sit on the bed. We hold hands.

We hear someone coming up the stairs. We wonder about hiding. But it is too late. She comes into the room. Here they are! she calls to someone behind her. Come! she says to us. Come! And she takes our hands, pulls us up from the bed. We look at each other, we do not understand, but she gives us no choice. Here they are! she cries as she leads us back down the stairs. I have them! she says as she pushes us gently into the other room, where the music is loud, where everyone is dancing.

Someone turns down the music and everyone is looking at us, swaying and smiling. They open up a space and there we are, in the middle of the room, surrounded by everyone, smiling, swaying. We look at each other. We grip hands. We do not understand.

The woman who has brought us down here, who took us from the coat-room and brought us, says, Will you please? Please... give us some? Some of your words! Your bio-chemistry words! And the others, the mathematicians and the physicists, the experimentalists and the theoreticians, the elderly Nobel prize-winner, they are all nodding, saying, Yes, yes, give us your words! Your words!

We are shy. We are holding hands, in the middle, the music still playing, everyone swaying. We look at each other. We wait. Is this real? we think. Do they really want this?

And then we do it. We begin. We say: DNA.

DNA! They all say. DNA! DNA!

Then we say, lymphocyte.

Ooh! They say, and they repeat the word. Lymphocyte, they say, turning to one another, still swaying. Lymphocyte!

Organelle, we say, and then: lamellipodia.

Lamellipodia! they cry and someone raises up her arms. The woman who brought us here, took us from the coat room, claps her hands. Lamellipodia! she cries. We look at each other. We smile a little. We loosen our handhold. Then we say, Green Fluorescent Protein.

Oh my! says the elderly Nobel prize-winner, and he does a twirl and then says Green Fluorescent Protein! The words ripple around the room until everyone is whispering them, chanting them. Green fluorescent protein, green fluorescent protein, and the chant becomes louder and louder. Someone turns the music up and then everyone is dancing.

We stand in the middle of the sea of dancing mathematicians and physicists, experimentalists and theoreticians, and the twirling elderly Nobel prize-winner, listening as they murmur Green Fluorescent Protein as they sway and dip. We stand and we smile, we smile and smile. We feel wanted. We feel loved. We feel heard.

Acknowledgements

The quote from Conversation by Louis MacNeice is taken from Collected Poems (Faber & Faber, 2016) and reprinted with permission.

Thank you to the following publications and their hard-working and fabulous editors who published many of the stories in this book:

Ambit (God Glows); Bare Fiction (Missing My Liar); The Binnacle (Thin Ice); Butcher's Dog (Hold the Baby); Catapult (Octopus's Garden); Commonwealth Broadcasting Association Short Story Prize 2008 (Straight Up); Edgeways anthology (Spread the Word) (Flavours); The Fiction Desk Prize Anthology (A Call to Arms); Five Dials (The Special Advisor); kill author (All Activity Is Silent); Litmus: Short Stories From Modern Science (Comma Press) (We Are All Made Of Protein But Some Of Us Glow More Than Others); The Lonely Crowd (But If I Knew A Little More); Metazen (It Begins With Birds in Flight, Burrowing Blind); National Flash Fiction Day Anthology (Stopwatching, If Kissed By A Dragonfish); Nature Futures (The Perfect Egg); New Flash Fiction Review (The Most New Sport); New Scientist magazine (Experimentation); Out of Place anthology (Spineless Wonders) (The Evolutionary Imperative Of Laughter Is Confused); Prose Poem Project (A Scar

Sits Above My Heart); The Red Room anthology (Unthank Books) (A Shower of Curates); Room magazine (The Party); r.kv.r.y (Dissolving); Salt Book of New Writing 2013 (A Song For Falling); Schemers Anthology (Stone Skin Press) (The Plan or You Must Remember This); Synaesthesia magazine (Biography); STILL anthology (Negative Press) (Switchgirls); Stinging Fly (Fine as Feathers, Against Joy); Stories for Homes anthology I (Something Like A Tree); Timber journal (Tunnelling); Wales Arts Review (War Games); Words with Jam (The House of Meat); World Literature Today (Empty But For Darwin)

Thank you also to: The Verb, BBC Radio 3, for commissioning What Is It That Fills Us; BBC Radio 4 for commissioning Experimentation; Sara Davies for commissioning The Party for Made in Bristol for Radio 4; Sweet Talk for commissioning There Is No-One In The Lab Tonight But Mice for Radio 4; the Royal Literary Fund for commissioning And What If All Your Blood Ran Cold; A J Ashworth for commissioning A Shower of Curates for the Red Room Bronte-inspired short story anthology; Spread the Word, for commissioning Flavours for the Edgeways London Short Story Prize anthology; Roelof Bakker for commissioning Switchgirls; Spineless Wonders for commissioning The Evolutionary Imperative Of Laughter Is Confused for the Out of Place anthology; and Stone Skin Press for commissioning The Plan or You Must Remember This.

Thank you to Hawthornden Castle for the month's writing residency in 2011 where a number of these stories were finished and others begun. An enormous thank you to Jon Keating, then Dean of the Faculty of Science at the University of Bristol, who appointed me writer-in-residence, and to Paul Martin and Kate Nobes, in whose laboratory at the University of Bristol I was writer-in-residence in 2010, a residency which inspired many stories in this collection. Thank you to the members of the lab (Becky, Mathieu, Jonno, Lucy, Will, Debbie, Rob, Yi, Yutaka and Dawn) who indulged my questions and allowed me to watch – and sometimes pick up a pipette myself. Thanks also to Phillipa Bayley, then at the Office of Public Engagement at the University of Bristol, who was a fantastic resource and source of enthusiasm.

Thank you to Robin Jones and Ashley Stokes at Unthank Books for making this beautiful book and for everything you do for writers and for the short story. Thank you to Kate Johnson for being the friend and literary agent I had given up hoping for and was so delighted to find. And thank you to all the scientists and to curious people everywhere. Keep asking questions.